NOT DARK

A NOVEL BY BERIT ELLINGSEN

YET

Two Dollar Radio
Books too loud to ignore

TWO DOLLAR RADIO is a family-run outfit founded in 2005 with the mission to reaffirm the cultural and artistic spirit of the publishing industry.

We aim to do this by presenting bold works of literary merit, each book, individually and collectively, providing a sonic progression that we believe to be too loud to ignore.

Two Dollar Radio
Books too loud to Ignore

COLUMBUS, OHIO
For more information visit us here:
TwoDollarRadio.com

Cover: *The Horsehead Nebula*, ESO
Author photograph: Alexander Chesham

1

SOMETIMES, IN BRANDON MINAMOTO'S DREAMS, he found a globe or a map of the world with a continent he hadn't seen before. When that happened, a flash of excitement ran through him and he hurried on to explore the new place. Now he had the same feeling of sudden, unexpected discovery, and started running down the fir-shaded hill, stubbed one boot against a stone, stumbled in the soft, rain-sodden ground, nearly fell, and slid the remaining distance to where the grass-covered slope ended in a short overhang of roots and straw. In the pebble-strewn stream that ran beneath the beard of vegetation, he nearly twisted his ankle, making his ninety-liter backpack wobble and the steel canteen bang against his hip, nearly toppling him. But finally, he stood before the blue door on the wooden terrace, his boots caked with mud, his heart beating hard, and the air fragrant with the scent of pine sap and heather and earth. While he caught his breath, he took in the red walls, the unpainted deck, and the gabled roof where the dark eyes of solar cell panels gleamed even in the overcast day.

He felt weightless, only the pressure against the soles of his feet signaled the substance of the rest of his body. The cabin, the heath, the world shone inside him, in an intimate, shared existence. He closed his eyes and there was no body, and no world either, only the simple, singular nothingness he recognized as himself.

When his breath was less ragged and he could focus on something else other than gaining air, he took out his wallet and unzipped the pocket in the back where a small key bulged the brown leather. He pushed the key into the rust-spattered lock and turned it once. It didn't shift. He tried one more time, putting more weight on the key. The door held an antique ebony handle and had been painted a clear, deep hue without having been sanded down first, leaving craters and fault lines from multiple layers of pigment visible in the surface. A diamond-shaped pane of unevenly sealed glass sat high in the wood, but the window was dark and revealed nothing of the inside. He closed one hand around the handle and rattled the door while using the key with his other hand. The lock didn't turn this time either, but the door snapped back into its unpainted frame. He gave the door a good push and tried the key again, and this time the lock gave way. He shook his hand from its tight grip on the narrow metal and returned the key to his wallet. Then he pushed with both hands on the handle. The wood creaked open and swung wider to invite him in.

He stooped to avoid the frame and closed the door. Further inside the ceiling grew higher and more accommodating, with more than enough room for him to stand at his full height.

The interior of the cabin was a single space, about five meters in the short dimension and eight on the long. The floor was covered with wide hardwood planks the color of dried blood, edged with fake black nails painted at the ends. He almost laughed when he saw it. The maritime-style ship-deck floors had been popular some years ago, in executive offices, high-end stores, and newly built apartments, but then fallen harshly out of fashion. It had been a long time since he had encountered one. The former owners must have bought the flooring on sale or acquired it from another building, and transported it all the way up to the heath, far away from the ocean and the maritime look alluded to.

All four walls lacked baseboards and the northwest corner missed covering, but a few planks had been left on the floor. If there were tools in the cabin's lean-to shed the corner would be easy to fix. Otherwise, he'd buy a hammer, saw, and nails the next time he hiked through the heather to the nearest town. The cabin smelled of dust with an undertone of mold. He inspected the walls and ceiling, but found no stains of moisture or blotches of fungi.

The long wall to the east was occupied by the kitchen and consisted of a few cupboards in a delicate eggshell blue, a laundry sink in steel of a type he recognized from his grandparents' old house on the eastern continent, a small refrigerator at the end of the worktop, and a gas stove with a fat canister of propane gas beneath it. The kitchen was illumined by a rectangular window above the sink, the dim afternoon light bounded by once-white frilly curtains. On the floor was a rug made from rags in primary colors, the old fabric now tangled with dust. The stove was a large four-ring camping cooker mounted on a wooden frame. He hunched by the canister and sniffed. He detected no leakage, but he'd have to check the gauge and tubing in full daylight. The fridge was empty, but clean, a power cord curling to the socket in the wall behind. The cupboards held stacks of plain white plates in two sizes, large and small, and cups and saucers in the same non-patterned design. Some of the glassware was cracked and chipped at the edges. The drawers by the sink contained a red mesh tray of stained cutlery and some dented pots and pans, all gray with dust and the sticky remnants of spider webs. The kitchen ended at the blue-painted door that led to the deck outside.

A tripartite panorama window took up almost the entire west

wall, looking out on the moor and the mountain range that constrained it. Dusk had almost swallowed the sky, and dark clouds rushed toward the distant peaks. The draft from the three large windows was palpable, even in the middle of the room. The white frame was gray with dust and the sill beneath it littered with curled-up spider husks and desiccated flies. There were some mouse feces as well, and lumps of brown fur, but he neither saw nor heard any other signs of rodents.

By the north wall stood a sagging three-seat sofa with printed purple poppies the size of human heads, and a long, frilly skirt. Leaning against the south wall was an old lime-green spring mattress. When he touched its surface dust whirled up, yet the smooth fabric seemed dry and free of mildew. He went over to the door, opened it to the dimming evening, and carried the mattress to the deck. There he hit the fabric repeatedly to get the worst of the dust off, then stood the mattress on end and bounced it a few times. More particles left to spread on the evening breeze. He sneezed, slapped the mattress some more, then carried it back inside and shut the door against the coming night.

2

BY THE PANORAMA WINDOW WAS A SQUARE PIT IN
the floor, filled with lumpy sand. Above it, a bronze hood shaped
like the bulb of an onion hung suspended from the ceiling, vent-
ing to the roof. A hearth, but with modern ventilation. Although
he had seen pictures of the cabin's interior and exterior, the fea-
ture surprised him. In the corner by the pit was a single electrical
outlet, which must be connected to the solar panels on the roof.

He creaked across the floor and sat down by the hearth. The
sand was dense and caked, not fine and loose as in the traditional
houses of his father's country. He passed his fingertips over the
grains like one might water. Something moved in the dark mass
and he pulled his hand back. A red centipede, as long as his
palm, rushed up from the sand, and vanished into the gap in the
northwest corner. He inspected the wool insulation. A tiny crack
in the siding brightened to the heather outside, and he hoped
the centipede had fled there instead of further inside the wall.

He returned to the hearth and sat there for a good while.
When it was almost dark he went outside in the drizzle and
pulled a few branches off the tree closest to the deck. It turned
out to be a dried-up magnolia, presumably planted by the cabin's
former owner. The twigs carried the remnants of a few flower

buds and leaves, long since yellowed and decayed by the fall. The sky above the low peaks on the other side of the heath was black with gathering clouds.

The branches were covered in a fine layer of dried mud and were humid to the touch, but he stacked them in the hearth and held the flame of his camping lighter close to them until they finally caught fire. The light flickered over the night-dark walls and exhaled small breaths of heat which only emphasized the chill in the rest of the room. When the fire had consumed the wood he didn't go outside to replace it, but undressed to his t-shirt and boxer briefs, pushed the mattress to the hearth, rolled his thin sleeping bag out on it, and fell asleep, even though it was barely six o'clock in the evening.

The next morning he put on running pants and trainers and went out on the deck. The air was sharp and fresh, easily bypassing his single layer of fabric, stealing the heat from his body, but the sensation only made him more alert. Far to the southwest and northwest were the neighboring farms: wooden houses, barns, courtyards, gardens. Except for them the moor held only heather and wild grass. He drank in the bright autumn light, the cold wind, the smell of vegetation and soil, and it felt like something sublimated and left him. He leapt from the unpainted deck and into the flowering heather, the ground firm and dry, not soft and sodden like he had expected, and began to run.

He continued west down the slope of the plain, feeling like he could run all the way to the summits in the distance. It made him think of a story he had read, about a dead man and a blackbird who traveled through a decaying, atrophied world to reduce the heat from the sun. Because the man was dead he needed no rest, and the two crossed a wide moor for days before they ascended into the mountains. Now he wanted to do the same, continue without stop until he reached the round blue peaks that bordered the moor. It looked like it would take at least two days of running. He wasn't back to that level yet, so it would provide him with a nice goal for the future. He tried to remember which town or county lay on the other side of the peaks, but failed to recall a mental map of the region, his mind unwilling to hold onto anything but the mountains and the heather and the fragrance of the heath.

When the sun glimmered above the peaks, the slanting rays stung his eyes and warmed his skin. The silvery morning light made him feel transparent, clear as glass. He squinted and grinned and ran on in the bright morning until the cabin and its small outhouse were dark spots behind him, and he seemed to be equally distant from it and the peaks. Then he continued back through the vegetation for a long while and arrived at the cabin just as the sun completed its brief autumnal arc in the sky and started falling behind the mountains.

3

HE THOUGHT HIS ARRIVAL ON THE MOOR HAD gone unseen, but the next day people appeared. From the mattress by the hearth he saw shadows moving behind the curtains in the kitchen window. He let the visitors do whatever they wished and pretended not to notice. He wasn't doing anything that was interesting to watch anyway.

"I see a ghost in there," a child commented through the door. Someone shushed her and retreated from the deck, their steps shivering the old planks.

"The natives are restless," he texted Michael.

"Be careful," Michael wrote back.

"Always," he replied.

"When are you coming back home?"

"I just got here."

"What does the cabin look like?"

"Not bad. As in the photos."

"I miss you," Michael wrote.

"I'll be home again soon," he replied, with no other reassurance than that.

The next day there were even more people, three middle-aged men and a woman, who knocked quietly on his door and introduced themselves as Eric, Pieter, Mark, and Eloise, neighbors. He shook their hands and returned their smiles and let them inside. They filed into the cabin, cluttering the entrance with their shoes, spreading the smell of sweaty feet and the sound of steps on the blood-red hardwood floor. Then they squeezed together on the dusty sofa with pained looks on their faces, while he apologized for the lack of additional seating.

He took out some mugs from the cupboard and asked the guests if they wanted tea. At first they declined, but then they said yes, that would be lovely, so he had to turn on the gas and light the stove and rinse the dusty cups in the sink and heat water in the dimpled kettle and take out some tea bags from his backpack and talk.

"Who are you, where are you from, what are you doing here?" they asked, but in more roundabout terms. He told them that he was from a city south along the coast and that he had recently bought the cabin and its plot. The visitors were from the neighboring farms and after a while he gathered that they wished to lease his land for an agricultural project. They must already have decided that he was no farmer and unlikely to attempt to grow anything on his own.

"You really want to rent the heath?" he nearly blurted out, but stopped himself in time and just said, "Yes, yes, yes."

They smiled and said, "We'll come over again soon and tell you more about our plans."

When they left, he crawled to the panorama window to remain out of sight.

"That wasn't so difficult," one of the men said as they sauntered down toward the farms in the southwest.

"Mind your chatter," came the reply.

He huffed and crept back to the fading fire in the hearth. The moor was only heather and low shrubs. Wasn't it too cold, the soil too barren to grow anything here?

4

THE CONTINENT'S SPACE ORGANIZATION WAS
seeking new recruits for their manned exploration program. It
was mentioned in the news only briefly, one story among dozens
of others, soon drowned out by subsequent news cycles, but to
him it stood out. Those selected as astronauts might be among
the first humans to land on Mars. Since most space projects took
decades to advance from the first concept to the final launch,
the space organization must be well underway in developing the
technology and experience needed for the trip.

He sat on the fake ship floor with the laptop plugged into the
single outlet from the solar panels on the roof. He had yearned
to go to Mars since he was old enough to understand the concept of other worlds. It didn't matter if the place was inhospi-
table and remote, had too little air and was too cold and dry. The
desire to travel there remained the same. He did wonder if the
challenges of cosmic radiation, lack of nutrition, loss of bone
and muscle mass, and weakening of the immune system that
would happen during the long journey to Mars and back had
been solved, and searched for information on the space organization's web pages. He found few answers, but nevertheless
returned to the application page and filled out the information

the space organization wanted, storing the form online to send later.

Lastly, he took a visual and spatial perception test necessary for the application; he predicted the next geometric shape in a sequence, rotated variously colored blocks in his mind until he could almost reach out and turn them with his hands, and read the numbers off black and white square and round gauges while a timer in the corner rushed the seconds away. When he was done it had grown dark and the log from the wood he had bought in the town center earlier in the day had died out in the hearth. He switched the laptop off, texted Michael goodnight, undressed, and curled up inside the sleeping bag.

"I'll let you leave on one condition," Michael had said the last night before he left for the cabin.

He turned on the pillow toward Michael. "I will come back. I promise."

"It's not that," Michael said.

"OK, what is it, then?"

Michael drew a breath. "That you text me 'Goodnight and I love you' every night before you go to sleep."

He looked at Michael. By now he must know he loved him.

He spent the days running and hiking on the moor, forming various routes around the islets of birches, mounds of bilberry, and troughs of cloudberry and cup lichen interspersed in the heather. When he needed more food and firewood, he walked to the town center. In the evenings he watched the news and popular science documentaries on the laptop while it used the power harvested from the sun.

He read about the Hercules-Corona Borealis Great Wall, the largest structure the astronomers had found so far in the universe, a wall of filaments of galaxy clusters ten billion light years across. In its brightly glowing web each tiny point of light was not a star, but an entire galaxy containing billions and billions of stars, many with their own planets, moons, and asteroid fields. He tried to imagine something as large and encompassing as the Hercules-Corona Borealis Great Wall, but it was so impossible, so unimaginable, that he had to go outside on the deck and see for himself the stars that gleamed above the heath.

The next morning the neighbors were there again, as they had said they would be, the two youngest, bringing with them a barking, medium-sized dog on a leash. He told them to leave the pet outside and invited them in.

"Would you like some tea?" he said, like last time.

"Yes, please," they said, like last time.

He padded to the kitchen and filled the kettle with water. The faucet gargled and spat a few times before it ran smooth with clear, clean water. He put the old steel on the stove and lit the blue-burning gas with a match. As he handed the visitors their cups, one of the glass containers slipped from his hands, spun upward, and started on a trajectory toward the floor. Before he had time to think, his body had already reacted, caught the cup with open palms, and handed it to them. They grinned and cheered. He smiled, fetched the kettle and the tea bags, poured the hot water into their waiting cups, and sat down on the floor in front of them.

"We plan to use the change in climate to grow barley, rye, and wheat, low-pH winter varieties, of course," the thirty-something woman who he remembered had introduced herself as Eloise, said. "That's what our project is about."

"But there's just heather and mud here," he said.

"It's become a lot warmer than it used to," her companion, Mark, said. "With the right treatment and seeds, the moor will be fertile enough."

He thought of the Hercules-Corona Borealis Great Wall and how it contained everything that was possible, all that could exist in its part of the universe, connecting it with the rest of the cosmos, leaving out nothing, accepting everything.

"I will let you use the land," he said. "For free. Just give me a little of whatever it yields."

"That's a deal," Eloise said and held out her hand. "Thank you so much. We will give you our contract and copies of the research and preparations we have done on the project, as well as the monthly progress reports we make for our investors."

"I'm looking forward to seeing them," he said. He shook their hands one by one, a warm and sturdy pressure against his skin.

"So you'll be staying then?" Mark, Eloise's husband, said.

"Yes," he said. "At least for a while."

5

FROM THEIR PRONE POSITIONS BEHIND A HALF-
crumbled wall, Kepler gave him the wind speed, wind direction,
and distance to the far edge of the dirt road a few hundred
meters ahead and six floors below them. The distance differed
slightly from the number he had measured himself.

"You must be joking," he said and disputed the result to see
if he could work Kepler up a little, although he knew the spotter
was right and adjusted his sights accordingly.

There was plenty of time. They had set out early and he had
driven Kepler hard through the burned-down, bombed-out
streets, past the vehicle cadavers and the mounds of debris, to
the third tallest building that was still standing on their stretch
of the road, and up through the gutted, wind-shorn structure.
He wondered how Kepler had made it through the intense training required by the special unit, because the man huffed and
puffed even after short lengths of travel and occasionally had
problems concealing himself because of the size of his body.
For that reason he sometimes chose routes through the rubble
he knew would tire Kepler and had smaller or narrower hiding
places, but the man was so observant he always found a wall seg-
ment or pile large enough to hide behind, and had the emotional

resilience not to complain to him about it. Today, Kepler had been panting the whole time, but when the spotter set the booby traps in the stairs below, it had been with calm and steady hands.

Kepler lifted his rangefinder binoculars without moving any other part of his body and repeated the distance he had measured earlier with a confidence born from careful consideration and long-time experience, not simply stubbornness or the need to be right.

"Where the hell are you pointing that thing?" he replied.

"At your dick, or I wouldn't be able to see it," Kepler said and laughed from deep inside his belly.

"Someday, Kepler," he said, "you'll make a good spouse for another man."

"I suppose you would know," Kepler said and laughed again.

He had been open about his sexual orientation; he wasn't the only one in the unit, and he thought he'd be able to handle any idiot remarks. The others had been surprisingly open-minded and made fewer comments and jokes than he'd expected, although one or two kept their distance, especially during social events or nights off. Kepler had made no such move and remained outgoing and talkative with him. That annoyed him too, that Kepler was more tolerant of him than he was of Kepler.

They watched in silence. At midday the wind rose and swept down the wide river valley and through the eviscerated building, stirring up sand and dust, and rolling tiny pieces of rubble over the ledge beyond. At most patrols nothing happened. Maybe a convoy or two, civilian or coalition, passed by on the road, or a dog or a fox slouched along the ditch that separated the thoroughfare from the desiccated field behind it.

Once, a rodent-like animal three times the size of a rat, with a broad, round back and a long naked tail, appeared right after twilight. Its whiskers had been bristling, its snout groping, and the fur slick with sewage.

"What the fuck is that?" Kepler had said. "Shoot it, shoot it!"

"Don't be stupid," he said. If the crack from the shot didn't give them away, the flash most certainly would. He hadn't wanted to risk that, yet it had been difficult not to put a round into the disgusting animal. When they returned to camp, Kepler told everybody about the "giant rat" which his shooter had been too kind-hearted to kill. The other teams tallied scores and competed against each other; now their teasing for making Kepler and him join the contest only increased.

In the early afternoon a police truck rumbled past on the road, kicking up a veil of dust which hung in the air for a long time. A few hours later the vehicle returned, going in the other direction.

Then an old man and a donkey pulling a small cart appeared on the dirt, moving slowly along the parallel depressions left from countless wheels. The donkey flicked its ears and swished its tail while it blinked with endless animal patience. The cart's load was covered with worn tarp, bulging from the objects beneath it.

"What have you got in that cart, grandpa?" Kepler muttered.

Both the man and the donkey were gray-haired and rheumatic-looking and moved at an infinitesimal pace along the road. The man wiped moisture from his deeply wrinkled face with a plaid handkerchief and flies buzzed around the animal's muzzle. When the two had passed the midpoint of their field of view, the man stopped the donkey, glanced around, hobbled over to the cart, and lifted the edge of the tarp. Both Kepler and he froze on their glass. The old man took something they couldn't see out from the cargo and crouched behind the cart.

"Is he in cover from you?" Kepler said.

"No," he said. "The top of his head is just above the edge."

"Will that be enough?"

"Yes."

Kepler gave him the distance and windage to the upper

railing of the cart, he adjusted, and took the final aim. But then the donkey shifted sleepily on its hooves and pulled the vehicle ahead a few steps, revealing that the man's activities behind it were entirely peaceful, if very private, and that the object he had taken out was a bottle of water to use afterward.

"In all the holy hells!" Kepler laughed and lowered his range-finder. "That would have sounded good in the debrief, killed civilian while he was taking a crap!"

He laughed too, against his will.

After the old man and the donkey had vanished, only dust stirred up by the breeze moved along the road for a good while. In the late afternoon four women appeared, carrying water in scuffed plastic cans, infants on their arms, toddlers clutching their hands, with slightly older children plodding behind them. Some of the youngsters clenched loaves of bread in their dirty hands.

"Pew pew!" Kepler said while staring into the binoculars, then gave him the distance and windage of the passing group.

"Oh, please," he said.

"What?" Kepler said. "They'll grow up to be enemy fighters."

"I'm hungry," Kepler said an hour after the women and children disappeared. One more hour and Kepler took out and unwrapped a protein bar, bit off a generous piece, and held out the rest to him.

"No," he said, "I don't want any."

Kepler moved the bar a little closer and waved it so the smell of cereal and sugar reached him.

He broke off the end, chewed slowly, could barely get it down.

Kepler held the food out to him again.

Once, he had gotten heatstroke from the sun and low blood sugar, and fainted in position. Kepler had doused his head and neck with drinking water and fireman-carried him back to the camp. The last thing he remembered from that trip was hanging limply over Kepler, vomiting on the spotter's shoulder, and Kepler saying: "Hang on, we'll be there soon."

They took turns to get up and stretch and relieve themselves in a corner in the next room. When they were out on nights off Kepler for some reason refused to use public toilets, and as a result had a bladder which seemed to contain liters, but outdoors and in the rubble the man had no such compunctions. He, on the other hand, loathed the patrols where he couldn't move and had to do his business where he lay, like a wild animal, and returned to the camp stinking as one.

"They're not even trying today," Kepler said. "Have we put the fear in them for good?"

"Just wait till it gets dark," he said.

The sky turned more and more fiery before the sun dropped behind the mountains on the other side of the valley. He missed the bright, protracted dusks of home.

Several hours after nightfall there was movement on the road. In the night vision optics four figures were clearly visible. They were carrying backpacks and bags and moved quickly along the ditch on the far side of the thoroughfare. Kepler remained quiet. The group was several hundred meters away, but sound carried far in the rural quiet. The four figures stopped and put their loads down. Two of them peeled open the bags, while the others rose and started digging with hand shovels in the old wheel tracks on the road. Something looked odd about the four, but he couldn't tell exactly what. Then he realized they were very young, perhaps only eleven or twelve, just a few years older than the children they had watched scamper after the women earlier in the day. He watched them intently. Kepler had not given him the range, but the group remained close to where the old man had stopped, and he could easily calculate the number himself. At sundown the evening had been almost windless, and as far as he could tell, the breeze had not picked up since then.

He glanced at Kepler. The spotter was watching the children through the binoculars, breath rapid and uncontrolled. He sank back behind his scope. Now the two with the bags had extracted the contents completely, large objects sprouting a profusion of wires. Slowly and carefully, the boys picked one device up between them and started carrying it over to the shallow hole the two others had made in the ground.

"Distance?" he whispered.

No reply.

"Kepler," he hissed.

"I'll call it in after," Kepler said. "The mine crew can..."

"I'm not risking that," he said.

Silence.

"Distance," he said. Two pairs of hands started lowering the first device into the hole.

"They're just children," Kepler hissed. "Are you really going to shoot all four of them?"

"No," he said, exhaled, and entered the space between one breath and the next.

The round curved out of the muzzle, glowing faintly on its trajectory like a falling star. Then the wired object exploded, with a pop more than a bang, which nevertheless tore the night apart. Almost immediately, the first detonation was followed by a second, the other device going off in the shockwave from the first. Then the fire and smoke from both flared in his sights. He scanned the ground for the dead. Only a few scattered remains were left of the two that had been burying the device. The others had been digging close by when the explosive went off. There they were, still alive, but something was clearly wrong. They weren't trying to crawl or roll away from the debris that was falling and smoldering around them. Instead they were writhing and gasping on the ground, clawing at their eyes and foaming at the mouth. For a second he didn't understand what had happened.

"What the hell?" Kepler said, still behind the binoculars.

"Gas," he said. "From the devices."

"Jesus," Kepler said, snapping for air.

"Time to leave," he said, looking up from the scope and pushing the night vision goggles on his helmet down.

"No," Kepler said, tugging at his sleeve like a little boy. "We have to help them!"

"Their friends will be there soon."

"At least put them out of their misery!"

"What?" he said.

"Look. Look!" Kepler flipped his goggles back up and pushed the binoculars down in front of his face, banging it hard into his upper lip. In the green illumination in the rangefinder the two surviving boys were still moving.

"If I shoot them now," he hissed while pushing the binoculars away, "that will be even worse! Killing injured civilians, not giving them a chance to get help. Even you must understand that!" Before Kepler could stop him, he pushed off from the ground, shouldered his weapon, and started toward the stairwell.

Behind him he heard the quiet shuffle of Kepler rising, picking up the backpack, and following him across the floor.

They relocated to another spot in the hope of capturing the people who had instructed the children to plant the devices, but no one came to the boys' aid. The road was empty, the night again dark and quiet, and they were told to return to the camp.

After the debrief neither he nor Kepler received a reprimand, but the previously frequent and intense goading to have them enter the kills contest stopped. Kepler carefully guarded his words around him and could barely meet his eyes. After he left the service, he didn't hear from Kepler again. He never told Michael or Katsuhiro or anybody else what he had done.

6

HIS FIRST TASK AS PHOTOGRAPHER FOR THE FAC-
ulty of natural sciences at the city's university had been to shoot
owls that were part of research into avian hearing and echoloca-
tion. He met Kaye, the assistant professor who had requested a
photographer, by the reception desk on the fifth floor of The
Institute for Biological Sciences. The assistant professor was a
healthy-looking man of medium height, with light brown curly
hair, and was somewhere in his mid-thirties, but his cargo pants,
fleece sweater, and worn hiking boots made him seem younger.

"We'll have to go up to the next floor," Kaye said.

"There was no 6 button in the elevator," he said.

Kaye gave him a glance. "The floor was added to the center
of the roof long after the building itself was complete. That's
why there are no elevators and the structure is not visible from
the ground."

"Oh, it's a secret government facility," he said.

"The government doesn't give a damn about zoology, or the
environment for that matter," Kaye said. "The sixth floor is
where we keep the animals used for research. It's not discussed
much, by staff or students, and not many people know about it."

"What sort of animals?"

Kaye shrugged. "Mice and rats mostly, a few rabbits and chickens, some bats, and of course, the owls. The rooms are small, though. That's why I want you to see them first, before you start carrying spotlights and cameras up."

"So how do we get there?"

"I'll show you," Kaye said, and began moving down the corridor. "Do you have any allergies? To mice or rabbits?"

He shook his head. "None."

"Any phobias of birds or feathers?"

"I ought to be able to handle that."

Kaye grinned. "Good, then I can show you to the owls."

He followed Kaye down a hallway painted in a nauseating green, with a well-waxed linoleum floor in the same institutional hue. Most of the doors were open and allowed glimpses into laboratories, offices, and storage rooms. Students and academic staff of various ages moved through the corridor, and a few nodded to the assistant professor as they passed.

"This way," Kaye said, turning first one corner, then another. At the end of the corridor three steps of grated stairs led up to an elevated door, which looked sturdier than the others in the hallway and was flanked by a keypad with metallic keys. Kaye typed a six-digit code into the keypad, then pulled the door open when the lock beeped.

"After you," the assistant professor said. A short flight of stairs surrounded by white walls led to another door with a keypad. Kaye used the same code and pulled the handle as soon as the lock sounded. Inside was a corridor in the same sickly green as the floor below, only narrower, lower, and with fewer doors. They were all closed, sealed shut with black rubber lining, and bearing keypads. In the ceiling, circular vents covered by shields of consecutively smaller and smaller rings created a strong downward draft.

They passed two doors. At the third Kaye stopped and

unlocked it with another six-digit code. When the assistant professor opened the door, air hissed into the room beyond.

"Good ventilation," he commented.

Kaye nodded. "Slightly lower air pressure than outside, so nothing escapes to the rest of the building. Animal allergens are bad for air quality."

"And viruses?"

"None that will infect humans," Kaye said with a wink, grinning white, even teeth at him.

The space they entered was small, barely two by three meters. The long walls carried a row of hooks, on which several white lab coats, a few dark ones, and several mint green coveralls hung. Beneath them were racks for shoes, empty, except for a cardboard box and a yellow plastic bag someone had left behind. In the ceiling, fluorescent lamps emitted a light that was so bright it was almost blue.

"Please put this on," Kaye said, handing him a green coverall and plastic shoe covers from the box.

He hung his short wool coat up and pulled the laboratory garment on. It was thin and crinkly and resembled paper, with the legs and sleeves ending in elastic bands.

The assistant professor removed his own brown fleece sweater, revealing a white t-shirt and a surprisingly solid physique underneath, and pulled on a coverall too. Kaye then took out a metallic red climber's carabiner bristling with keys of various sizes, picked one, and unlocked the next door.

The room inside was also long and narrow, with a worktop running the length of one wall. The white surface featured two steel sinks with large, curving faucets, the lens of a motion sensor beneath each steel neck, bottles of liquid soap and disinfectant next to them. Along the worktop were boxes of latex-free lab gloves in four sizes, a white plastic wash bottle labeled "twenty percent ethanol," and a glazed ceramic jar holding pens and markers of various thickness and colors, boxcutters, and a laser pointer. There was also a shallow plastic box containing hammers, tongs, an awl, scalpel handles, and a set of screwdrivers in various sizes. The shelves above the worktop had no doors and displayed stacks of plastic bowls and boxes, graded glass beakers, measuring cylinders, pipettes, square plastic bottles labeled "sodium chloride," "potassium chloride," and other salts, more hand disinfectant, and several brown glass bottles containing medical-grade ninety-eight percent ethanol. Beneath the worktop were rows of drawers and cabinet doors, as well as large bags of food pellets and wood wool, stacks of paper towels, and plastic buckets.

On the opposite wall were four rows of transparent plastic boxes lined with wood wool, a tube of liquid attached to each box. The scratched plastic dampened the brightness of the fluorescent light to a golden glow. Inside each softly illumined world small furry backs were curled up in the wood wool. The mice seemed to be asleep; no tiny mammal was jumping or running inside the plastic containers. Kaye didn't comment on the mice, but continued to the next door, where a large round shower head had been mounted on the wall. A triangular handle with an emergency sign dangled in a thin chain from the shower head. Beneath it, at chest height, was a circular steel bowl with a small tap and two rubber cups protruding from the bottom. The emergency shower and eye rinsing system was dusty and unused. Next to it was a plastic rack with first aid equipment behind a transparent lid.

In the room that followed the air was noticeably warmer, more humid, and smelled of pine trees and bird droppings. The space resembled most of all a dog pound, with tall cages of plastic-encased wire, stacked two on top of each other, in a row along the wall. Inside each enclosure perched an owl, as tall as the length of his lower arm, or larger. Some of the birds were white with dark speckles, others had a tan or gray base coloration over-laid with black or brown. A few of the owls turned their heads almost one hundred and eighty degrees to inspect their visitors with large, docile eyes, and blinked at them slowly, like cats, before they swiveled their heads back and ignored them. Others only shuddered and fluffed themselves a little, and shifted calmly on their perches.

Kaye grinned at him.

He smiled and approached the nearest cage.

"Magnificent, aren't they?" Kaye beamed.

He nodded and peered into one wire-bounded space, trying to meet the owl's gaze, but the large bird only winked a few times, closed its eyes, and remained still. "Are they all the same species?" he asked.

"No," Kaye said. "We have ten different species, because each navigates by auditory clues a little differently. Our aim is to study the full range of hunting techniques and neural wiring among owls, which is why we keep more than one species."

"Local ones?"

"From all over the world, but raised in captivity. Their wild cousins should be allowed to remain wild. These were saved from an aviary that had to close. They were born in captivity and couldn't be released without extensive training and care."

"What happened?" he said. "Lack of visitors?"

"A fire, a rather sudden one," Kaye said. "The park had a history of mistreating their birds. But the owls are happy now, that's what matters."

"Of course," he said.

Kaye continued to describe the owls, how the various species and their hearing differed and what significance that had for what type of prey they took and their rate of success.

He turned toward the other cages. "All I know about owls is that they're nocturnal."

"They're mostly active at night," Kaye said. "Or when they

perceive it's night, and that's when they usually hunt. But one or two species do hunt during the day if they need to, and they all do if the situation presents itself."

By the door to the next room hung a calendar with handwritten notes in red, blue, green, and black. The assistant professor leaned close to inspect it. "The owls have been outside today, but not fed their evening meal yet," Kaye said, "so I can show you that."

"Do you need me to do anything?" he said.

"Just watch. Think of it as introducing yourself, your voice and motions."

"Can they tell the difference between us?"

"Of course," Kaye said. "They are able to hear a mouse running through the underbrush in complete darkness with such accuracy that all they need to do is fly over and scoop it up with their talons."

"Soundlessly?" he said.

"Completely silent to us because of how their wings and tail are constructed," Kaye said. "They have to, since their prey is not only running, but also listening for its life."

"Amazing," he said.

"Isn't it?" Kaye said and gave him a broad smile.

The assistant professor returned to the room they just left. There he pulled out two laboratory gloves from a box and put them on. Then he took one of the mouse cages down from the rack and placed it on the counter. Inside the plastic several lumps of brown fur were visible in the wood wool.

Can't just feed one of the owls," Kaye said, "or the rest of them won't calm down for hours."

"Do they become envious of each other?" he asked.

"Who knows," Kaye said. "At least they can tell when someone else is getting something they don't and they dislike it. And why shouldn't they be capable of feeling envy, even if they are birds? They're intelligent enough to thaw food that's frozen over with the heat from their own bodies. Many animals seem to experience the same emotions as we do, joy, fear, anger, desire, and so on. Some even mourn their dead when they encounter a corpse of their own species."

"Really? I had no idea."

The assistant professor searched his face for a moment. "Sorry, I'm lecturing," Kaye said. "It's a bad habit, but almost unavoidable in academia."

"No, please go on."

"It seems that most, if not all, of our emotional responses are older than humanity," Kaye continued, a look of child-like eagerness on his face. "Much of what we think makes us human actually pre-dates us, our tools, and our civilization. We inherited love and altruism from our evolutionary forebears, those traits did not originate in human beings.

"Humanity is eradicating the habitats of millions of species, with several hundred going extinct each day. We've set off a new mass extinction, on a scale that's only happened five times before on the planet. Our hunger for non-renewable energy, cheap consumer goods, and endless economic growth is making the same impact on the environment as an asteroid would. Even worse, the large earth systems may be so destabilized that several aspects of climate change are now irreversible. It's impossible to say which wild animals or plants will survive under these conditions."

He looked at the assistant professor, not certain how to respond.

"Well, that concludes tonight's class," Kaye smiled. "Shall we get to work?"

Kaye carried the box of mice into the owl room and continued to the uppermost cage in the corner furthest from the door. The mottled gray bird that sat inside turned its head toward them and blinked, but did not otherwise move or make a sound. The assistant professor pushed one hand beneath the plastic lid of the mouse box and picked up one of the round forms that was sleeping inside the scuffed world. The mouse stirred only a little. With the other hand, Kaye slid the small latch of the owl cage aside, opened the door, and placed the mouse inside. In the new and unfamiliar environment the mouse kept to the walls of the enclosure and nearly vanished in the deep wood wool. The owl stretched its neck and moved its head from side to side. Then the bird hopped down almost nonchalantly and landed right on top of the mouse. The tiny mammal squeaked more loudly than its size indicated it was capable of and began to struggle intensely, but that could not save it from the owl's talons. The owl picked the mouse up with its beak and flapped back to the perch. There it tilted its head, snapped its mandibles a few times to orient the prey, stretched its neck, and devoured the mouse whole. The owl swallowed a few more times, shook its feathers, then closed its large yellow eyes. The other birds were hooting, turning their heads, and beating their wings so feathers and wood wool swirled inside the cages.

"Don't worry," Kaye said. "We do have a special permit to feed the owls live mice."

He nodded. He had seen worse, of course he had, but he couldn't tell that to a stranger.

"I'd better finish this before all of them start shouting," Kaye said. The assistant professor continued to the next enclosure, dipped his hand into the mouse box, opened the latch, dropped a mouse inside, shut the wire door, then progressed to the next owl. As the birds spotted the mice, they fell silent, and chased and ate their prey.

"They don't receive the food for free though," Kaye said after he had fetched a second box of mice and fed all the owls. The assistant professor crossed the bird room and opened the door in the back. "This is where they earn their meals."

The room inside was square, about five by five meters, and lit by small, strong spotlights. The walls as well as the ceiling were paneled in a blue plastic material that was smooth and soft to the touch. The floor was covered with the same wood wool as the mouse boxes and owl cages. On the other side of the room was a rectangular mirror and a narrow door. In the center of the blue space stood an emaciated and nearly leafless birch tree. Gray and yellow droppings streaked the few branches that the tree possessed.

That's the problem with birds, he thought. They shit everywhere, even where they sleep.

Along the floor triangular sheets of green paper with white marker at the summits had been taped on the plastic surface. A few paper trees had also been glued to the walls to further mimic a place in the mountains, without making the illusion any more convincing. Instead, it looked like a rubber room for owls.

"We've tried to make it a little more homey for the birds," Kaye said, as if guessing his reaction. "But we haven't got much leeway because of the soundproofing and the microphone setup."

He nodded.

The assistant professor strode across the wood wool and unlocked the narrow door in the back. When he switched on the light inside, the mirror became a window. The small space was filled with two blond desks set at a right angle from each other, bounding a cluster of office chairs. The desks carried monitors, computer keyboards, and sound recording consoles, reminding him of the music studio Beanie worked at in the city center.

"This is where we measure the owls' hearing during the sound experiments," Kaye said.

He nodded at Kaye through the window.

"Listen to this," Kaye said. The assistant professor pressed one of the keyboards and a note played in the blue room. It sounded like the dull, amelodic tone of a hearing test. The silence that followed was thick and muted, nothing like the spacious, open quiet of the mountains. There was another note, longer and more high-pitched this time. Kaye pointed into the soundproofed room.

He turned to find out where the tone was coming from, somewhere in the corner to the left of the door. He went over to it and looked back at Kaye.

Kaye nodded and smiled, then played another sound, a deep one, which hummed right at the edge of his hearing.

He moved to the wall that emitted the tone.

The assistant professor grinned at him through the one-way mirror. "You're a good owl."

He smiled back.

"What do you think?" Kaye said, standing in the doorway. "Is the room too small for photographing the birds?"

He shook his head. "Should fit perfectly for a camera on a tripod," he said.

"Excellent!" Kaye said. "Then we're all set. Can we start tomorrow afternoon?"

"Yes," he said. "When?"

"Six," Kaye said. "Unless that's too late for you?"

"No, it's fine."

"I'll meet you at the door downstairs," Kaye said. "The foyer should be open until eight. If it's locked, just phone me."

He nodded.

The assistant professor went back to the recording room.

"It's rather late. Do you need a ride home?" Kaye said while switching the monitors and the lights off.

"Thanks, that would be nice," he said.

They exited the soundproof space and returned to the cloakroom.

"If you wish to be absolutely certain of not bringing any mouse allergens home, take a shower and wash your hair once you get there," Kaye said, peeling the green coverall off and putting on the brown fleece sweater again.

He nodded. "I'll probably go swimming."

"In the sea, at this hour?"

"No, there's a pool in the building."

"Really?" Kaye said. "And it's actually being used?"

"Mostly by me," he said. "I rarely see anyone else there."

"What a luxury," Kaye said.

He nodded.

They both exited, the door sighed shut and the lock whirred into place. The ventilation hummed. The hallway was dark, lit only by the green shine from an emergency sign at the end. When Kaye started down the corridor, the ceiling lamps flickered to life.

"Not many people up here," he said.

"No, not at this time in the evening," Kaye said. "Probably only a graduate student or two, doing overnight experiments."

They continued down to the fifth floor hallway and caught the elevator to the first floor. In the small mirrored space he leaned against the wall and avoided Kaye's eyes, listening instead to the whirring of the elevator as it moved through the shaft until it slowed, bounced, and the worn doors rattled open. The foyer of The Institute for Biological Sciences was empty. The rect-angular, rust-colored tiles on the floor dulled the light from the fluorescent lamps in the lowered ceiling that stretched from the elevators to the front door of the building. The rear wall faced an overgrown park and consisted of glass set in enormous rectangular wooden frames. In the space between the concrete front and side walls, and the glass-and-wood back, several suspended ramps rose toward the second and third floors. The panorama wall and ramps made the foyer look grand, but with the night pressing against the glass the space seemed dark despite the plentiful illumination. Their footfalls on the tiles were hushed and dry. The foyer was so beautiful he hoped he would never have to see it in full daylight.

Outside it was humid and foggy, on the verge of drizzle.

"My car's right over there," Kaye said and nodded at a modest vehicle further down the street. Except for the campus structures at the end, the thoroughfare was dominated by old yet well-kept tenement buildings which boasted elaborate casement windows, verandas with carved banisters, and tall finials at the gables. Kaye's car was cramped and old and smelled of gasoline and rain gear. The dashboard held a compact disc player and several unlabeled discs cluttered the small compartment beneath it. In the back seat unidentifiable clothing and a plastic bag lay rumpled.

"Please excuse the mess," Kaye said, got in on the driver's side, and pulled the seatbelt on.

"Where do you live?" Kaye asked.

"In the towers by the marsh."

"No wonder there's a pool in the building. All right, should be a quick drive."

"Where do you live?" he ventured.

"In the old part of the city, just south of the campus," Kaye said.

"Are you certain you don't mind driving so far out of your way?"

"It's not that far," Kaye said, smiling. "And at this time of night there's no traffic."

They drove in silence. The assistant professor seemed to have other things on his mind, and he felt no need to break the quiet. The sodium glow from the street lamps washed over the windshield in a regular, uninterrupted rhythm. Leaning into the headrest, he almost fell asleep, and only returned to attentiveness when the dry sound of the blinkers signaled that they were about to leave the motorway and enter the street toward the towers.

"These are some buildings," Kaye said, glancing up at the five nineteen-story structures that rose above them. "I remember when all this was wetland. My father used to hunt in the area. He once shot an owl and had it stuffed. I grew up with the poor thing on the mantel."

He smiled. "Is that a good memory or a bad one?"

Kaye laughed. "Bad, mostly, since the bird was dead. Which tower do you live in?"

"The second one."

Kaye stopped by the glass entrance to the second of the six-sided towers. "Do you want me to pick you up tomorrow?" the assistant professor said.

He shook his head. "Thanks, but no need. The trains from here go to the university."

"All right," Kaye said. "Have a good night and see you tomorrow."

"See you," he said, ignoring the sudden impulse to pull Kaye very close to inhale his breath and fragrance and ask him upstairs. Instead, he closed the car door quietly and continued to the gleaming entrance. He didn't look back, but followed Kaye's car as it came into sight and vanished down the slope to the motorway.

He didn't go swimming as he thought he would. Feeling unexpectedly tired, he took a quick shower to wash the scent of the owl room off, and went to bed. As soon as he lay still beneath the soft duvet, his two eastern-bred cats snuggled close, while their warmth and purring accompanied him to sleep. His dreams were filled with owls, but they were unable to fly, and ran across a dark forest floor on bare human feet.

7

HE CARRIED THE TRIPOD AND CAMERA BAG TO the fifth floor, and from there followed a windowed hallway to the staircase that led to the top level. That high up the night and the mist, which had been constant the whole spring and summer, cloaked the view of the park below. The formlessness that filled the glass was how he imagined being blind must feel. Not a complete darkness, but the absence of visual cues, a non-seeing. It made him want to turn toward the wall behind him instead, whose textures looked like clouds ought to, full of whorls and shapes and imaginary patterns.

Kaye arrived, smiling, carrying two paper cups with cardboard lids.

"Sorry I'm late," the assistant professor said. "Thought we could both be in need of the true fuel of our civilization." Kaye held one of the cups out to him, the scent of coffee rising with the steam. "I have packets of sweetener and non-dairy cream if you need it."

"Thank you, no, this is perfect," he said, took the cup, and shouldered the bag and tripod.

They continued upstairs to the sixth floor, through the hissing low pressure of the owl room's outer doors, to the blue light of the cloakroom, where they placed the coffee cups on the shoe racks while they changed into protective coveralls. He also wrapped shoe covers around the legs of the tripod. Kaye unlocked the door to the mouse room, the owl room, and the experiment room.

He put the tripod down and adjusted its legs. In the bag he had brought two short-distance and one low-light lens, along with the camera body and a remote timer.

"Looking good," Kaye said. "These images are the last things we need for a couple of new publications. As you probably know, in academia it's 'publish or perish.'"

"So I've heard," he said, scuffing away some wood wool with the tip of his shoe to make certain the legs were standing directly on the floor.

"Please take your time," the assistant professor said. "There's no rush. I'll let the owl in when you're done and we'll run the experiment right away."

"Anything in particular I should keep in mind?" he said, picking up his cup of coffee and looking at Kaye.

"Stand still as long as the owl is here," Kaye said. "The sounds I play will distract it so it shouldn't notice you. But if it does, don't panic. I'll keep an eye through the window. Oh, and put the camera on silent mode. It does have one?"

He nodded. "No problem."

"Good," Kaye said. "I'll wake up the computers." The assistant professor vanished through the slim door to the recording room.

The small soundproofed space with its paper mountains and cut-out trees was filled with the scent of wood wool and bird droppings. The silence in it was dense, compressed, he could even hear his own pulse. He chose one of the short-distance lenses from the bag and screwed it onto the housing, switched the camera on, removed the lens cap, and toggled the camera's shutter sound to mute. Then he pointed the camera at the tree and set the range so the whole room would be in focus since he didn't know where the owl would land. He switched the camera remote on and took a few test shots of the tree to adjust for the range and the light conditions. Finally, he set the camera to high speed photography and to capture several consecutive images with each click on the remote. When everything was done, he stepped into the corner behind the tripod, timer in hand, and squatted in the wood wool.

Kaye nodded at him through the window and exited. The assistant professor returned with a mouse box, which he carried into the monitor room, then left again. When Kaye next opened the door, a medium-sized brown and black owl was perched on his gloved right hand. Kaye moved quickly to the tree and held the owl close to one of the upper branches. After a moment's hesitation, the bird stepped over to the tree and settled. Kaye walked calmly but swiftly back to the monitor room and closed the door.

He waited and breathed. The owl was sitting with its back to him, but he nevertheless took a few shots of it. Then a deep, almost inaudible tone played somewhere close to the blue-padded ceiling. The owl reared up and spread its wings, which seemed to reach from one side of the small room to the other, flew to where the sound had emitted, before it banked and returned to the tree. Next, a higher pitched note appeared. The owl located the source of the new sound almost immediately. The tone after that had a similar pitch, but was played at an almost inaudible volume, yet clearly recognizable to the owl. Then the sound turned very sharp and high, almost painfully so. The next ones that followed must have been outside of his auditory range, because the bird lifted in a different direction twice without him hearing anything. Then came a few more tones, one medium pitched and loud, another low and quiet, almost like a rumble, which the owl located immediately and accurately. Finally, the door to the monitor room opened slightly and something rustled in the thick wood wool on the floor. The owl immediately took to its wings, as before in complete silence. He pressed the remote several times. Something bounced a few times in the shavings, then the owl returned to the barren tree with the catch secured in its talons and started to consume the mouse. Afterward, the bird moved its head from side to side a few times and adjusted its wings.

Kaye returned from the monitor room, glove on hand, and held it close to the owl's feet. There were no traces of the mouse left, not even tufts of fur in the wood wool. The owl turned its head a bit before it stepped onto Kaye's hand, talons sinking into the leather. The assistant professor stroked the soft, wide chest with one finger while keeping his gaze on the bird. The owl rolled its eyes and hooted. Then Kaye carried it back to the owl cages.

"How did it go?" Kaye said upon returning.

"I think it went very well," he said. "I took several pictures but will only know how they turned out when I've looked at them on a screen."

Kaye nodded. "Good," he said. "I have more owl species to photograph, but there's no point in doing that before we know how these are. Give me a call or text when you know."

"I will," he said.

"Are you in a hurry?"

"Not particularly. Just have to pack everything up."

"Give me a few minutes and I'll follow you outside. With the pictures coming along I need to finish the articles, so no more experiments tonight."

"Certainly," he said.

Kaye returned to the recording room and the lights went on inside.

He switched off the remote and the camera, returned the lens and the body to the bag, pulled the tripod's legs up, and folded them together. Through the glass he saw Kaye sip coffee while typing on one of the keyboards. After a few minutes the assistant professor returned, switched off the lamp in the monitor room, and locked the door.

"Ready to leave?"

He nodded.

They drove in silence as they had done the night before. The streets were empty and a chilly, lingering drizzle gave the street lights halos. All sounds were thick and distant, as if they were still in the soundproofed bird room. He could see the honeycomb towers shining in the distance, but they didn't seem to come any closer. Kaye continued along streets flanked by gabled houses with old-fashioned bay windows and carved door frames. Thick but neat hedgerows delineated the gardens from each other and the pavement outside. At a wooden house painted a bright orange-brown color, with black window frames and slim finials spearing the air from the roof, Kaye stopped the car. A low wrought-iron gate barred the short pathway from the pavement to the orange door, where a massive monkey puzzle tree loomed.

"Want to come in for a coffee?" Kaye asked.

He did.

8

INSIDE WAS A CLOAKROOM WHERE A DOOR WITH A
frosted window barred the way to the rest of the house. The
small space was held in a warm orange color, similar to the
exterior of the house, but a shade less intense. One side of the
cloakroom was draped with jackets and coats. He spotted at least
two down parkas, a navy-blue blazer, a black leather jacket, and
a pair of hardshell ski pants with suspenders. When he tried to
hang his own coat on top of one of the parkas, both fell off the
hook. He quickly lifted the clothes back in place, hoping Kaye
hadn't noticed. Below the outer garments stood a row of footwear: several mountain boots, a pair of tall rubber wellingtons, a
couple of sneakers, loafers, the rest hidden behind a leather bag
with shoulder strap, a canvas sports bag, and a red eighty-liter
backpack. He removed his shoes and placed them with the other
footwear.

The hall beyond the second door looked more like an old
woman's house than that of a young academic. The hardwood
floor had darkened with age and multiple applications of
varnish, its many eyes large and black. Four open doors with
thickly painted paneling and carved frames led out of the square
central space. A narrow set of stairs ascended to the second

floor, its wall covered with black and white images hung in dark frames, old photographs of relatives, he assumed. Among the pictures were also framed certificates and awards, like a display of achievements for the ancestors. At the bottom of the stairs stood a circular mahogany table covered with a round lace doily and an antique porcelain lamp painted with flax flowers.

"This used to be my grandparents' house," Kaye said. "I've been meaning to redecorate, but there never seems to be enough time. The living room and kitchen are a bit more this century, I promise."

He smiled. "Wait a few more years and this'll be trendy again."

Kaye laughed. "Want a drink?"

"Just some water, thanks," he said, hoping it wouldn't unnerve Kaye since his original invitation had included coffee.

"All right," Kaye said, hesitated for a moment, then turned and vanished through the door at the opposite end of the hall. "The living room's to the right, please make yourself at home!"

"Thank you," he said. He relished exploring new spaces, whether private or public, inhabited or abandoned. In the past, when he glimpsed from outside apartments or houses that were either too bare and lonely-looking, or crowded with old-fashioned, outdated furniture like here, he yearned to stand inside those rooms, to see and experience what whoever lived there did. He had even considered breaking into certain buildings for a closer look at what he could tantalizingly glimpse from outside. But in the end the obvious risks were too high for the possible reward, and he steered his tastes over to abandoned industrial places instead. Those were like open secrets, accessible if one only looked hard enough, and were often more interesting and beautiful than buildings that were still inhabited and maintained.

He nevertheless didn't want to miss the opportunity to look around in the old house before Kaye returned from the kitchen. He wanted to know more about the assistant professor without having to give away something about himself. Although he despised the self-aggrandizement of social media, he had searched for Kaye online. But except for a few websites at various research institutions which listed Kaye's academic credentials and publications, the assistant professor seemed to have as small an internet presence as he himself did.

The living room faced the back garden, where a rotary clothes line turned slowly in the darkness. The grass stood thick and tall from neglect and mild autumn weather. A low boxwood hedge separated the garden from the property behind it, another patch of lawn with another old house in the middle, this one in sky-blue stucco with white windows and doors. A black three-seat leather sofa stood against the window, holding a pile of laundry, clean from the crinkled look of it: t-shirts, socks, rumpled jeans and chinos, some underwear. In front of the sofa stood a blond oak table, covered in books and magazines, with even more stacked on the shelf beneath the top.

Opposite the window was a large shelf filled with books, ranging from small paperbacks at the top to hardbound volumes in the middle and large atlases at the bottom. Scattered on the shelves were carved figurines that looked tribal, framed butterflies and beetles, postcards from a rainforest and a polar landscape, a miniature head-mounted camera, a pair of pliers, a ring with several keys, and a flashlight. There was no TV, no DVD player, no music system, not even a radio. In the corner by the door stood a massive wood stove on an unpolished granite plate. The brass firewood holder next to it was three-quarters full of logs and the set of wrought iron spade and brush next to it were gray with soot. The doorway led to the kitchen, which he only glimpsed as a narrow space lined with cupboards.

The second door in the hall led to a dining room facing the front garden and the street. By the large bay window stood a dining table with eight chairs, made from a shiny burgundy wood he guessed was mahogany, carved into graceful legs and rails. Behind the table was a cabinet of the same material and design, its glass panes opaque with age. On the wall opposite the bay window hung a large oil painting with a frame as broad as his hand, carved into garlands and ribbons, the gilding having darkened with time. The canvas displayed a wetland devoured by black, roiling clouds that most of all resembled the front of a sandstorm. The sliver of sky above it looked like it was on fire. The bog itself lay in darkness, with the silhouettes of only a few trees and bushes visible. At first the painting reminded him of the tempests on Mars that could engulf the whole planet in dust, but with a sudden and irrational unease, he recognized the marsh as that which surrounded his apartment.

When Kaye appeared from the kitchen, he was sitting on the sofa next to the pile of laundry. The assistant professor put two steaming mugs of coffee down on the table, handle-less, with a geometric pattern along the rim. It reminded him of clayware he had seen in countries along the old trade route to the eastern continent, now impassable because of unrest and civil war. He was surprised, Kaye seemed so dedicated to his work he'd expected thermos mugs with the university's coat of arms.

"I made you some coffee anyway," Kaye said. "It's a chilly evening."

"Thanks," he said and smiled. The cup warmed his hands comfortably.

"Please ignore the mess." Kaye grinned, gathered up the pile of laundry, put it on the floor, and sat down.

He lifted the cup and inhaled the aromatic fragrance of the liquid. Refraining from blowing on it, he took a small sip. "It's good," he said, "but this will keep me awake all night."

"Is that a bad thing?" Kaye said and leaned very close.

At first the kiss was soft, but as he responded, it became more insistent. His pulse pounded in his ears and the rest of the world vanished in a rush of touch and scent and pleasure.

After that there were more evenings in the owl room, more coffee, and more nights in the old house. He didn't ask Kaye home and the assistant professor never invited himself there, perhaps for fear of being rejected. From the furtive glances Michael sent him when he thought he wasn't looking, he knew Michael suspected there was someone else. But from the unfamiliar scents on Michael and the lack of text messages, he also thought there was someone else with him. At least he hoped so, for his own bad conscience, but he never asked Michael.

He wondered what would happen when he was done photographing the owls. Would he see Kaye again, or would they quietly part ways? Was there even now an unspoken but definite agreement that when the job was done, that was it, or was there an expectation about something more, something longer lasting? Kaye didn't really seem interested in that, or he probably would have been more insistent. Or maybe the assistant professor was just busy and preoccupied with his work, as his house indicated. His own expectations were even harder to catch, like water in his hands, so he pushed the questions away till later.

At Kaye's there were images of friends, colleagues, grinning from university campuses and surfing beaches and mountain tops, and what looked like siblings, parents, grandparents, and other relatives, as well as a single photo of a blond man and a small child with the assistant professor. The man and Kaye looked like more than friends, seemed a family, but the print was unframed and dusty and lay on top of a pile of books on ecology and population dynamics on the floor in Kaye's bedroom. He didn't ask about the photo or any of the other mementos the house was filled with.

Once Kaye saw an image from the abandoned sanatorium he had explored last summer, of a rusted surgical table, pale stuffing bubbling out of rips and tears in the cushions, the broad foot speckled with corrosion and half covered in sand and leaves.

"What's this?" Kaye said and leaned closer to the screen.

It was too late to close the laptop, and if he did, the professor would probably just become more curious. He had to go with the questions.

"It's from the old sanatorium up north," he said. "Have you been there?"

Kaye shook his head. "No, but I've heard about it. Hasn't it been closed for decades?"

He nodded. "By the look of it."

"Did you take this?" Kaye said.

He nodded again.

"How did you get in?"

"Through the front door," he said. "It's fairly open."

"Fairly?" Kaye said, looked at him and laughed.

He smirked, but inside he was squirming at being asked about a place which felt so private.

"Does everything there look as ruined as this?"

"More or less."

"Did you go alone?"

"I did that time," he said. He didn't want Kaye to think he was a loner.

"Wasn't that risky?" Kaye said. "In such an old building far away from everywhere else?"

"Just a little," he said. He had broken four fingers on his right hand there, which required multiple plates and pins in the fractured digits, and several weeks in a cast, but the visit had nevertheless given him the impetus to seek employment as a photographer.

Kaye laughed, then took in the image again. "It looks brutal. And sad. Was it?"

"I guess it was," he said. "But beautiful too." It felt oddly good to have admitted that.

Kaye smiled. "Otherwise why go there to take pictures?"

"It reminded me of a place on the southern continent," he said and mentioned the name of the city where the casualties had been the greatest. He assumed the assistant professor would recognize it from the news.

Kaye grew serious but there was no sign of pity in his eyes, only warm interest. "Tell me more about it," the assistant professor said.

To his surprise he did.

9

HE DIDN'T KNOW HOW MANY PHOTOGRAPHS KAYE needed for his articles, but he had made several series of each owl, had become almost as familiar with their motion and energy as he was with the assistant professor's. He was waiting for Kaye by the stairs to the sixth floor. Someone had placed a worn bright-red office chair next to the door. He was clearly not the only person used to waiting there. The intensely colored furniture was a hard affair with armrests that wriggled when he sat down on it and upholstered in a particularly coarse and itchy wool.

Kaye appeared around the corner from the hallway that led to the elevators, shot him a lopsided smile, then climbed the grated stairs to the locked door. He grinned back at Kaye, rose from the sofa, and picked up the camera bag. They had spent the previous night in the bedroom on the second floor of the assistant professor's antique-looking house, without having worked in the owl room first. That had been unexpected, but felt too good to be alarming, at least for now. Kaye tapped in the key code and held the door open for him. As he passed the assistant professor and entered the stairwell, a warm hand traced his jawbone. He half turned and smiled before continuing up the steps.

The scents and sounds of the cloakroom, the mouse room, the owl room, and the auditory chamber, were now so familiar that they seemed ordinary, even comforting. As always when he was there, he wondered how he'd feel when the job was finished, and how much he would miss it. Kaye entered the recording room to turn on the computers and the sound equipment.

He set up his tripod and camera in the usual corner of the fake landscape and squatted with the camera remote in hand to wait for the assistant professor. Kaye exited the soundproofed room and returned with one of the largest owls sitting on his glove, a dark brown bird with bronze-colored eyes and long tufts of feathers that looked like ears on each side of its head, and lifted it to the tree to start the experiment.

Afterward, Kaye switched on the light in the recording room to signal that the experiment was over and that he could put the camera away. As he clicked the steel legs of the tripod together, there was a sudden beating of wings, a quick motion in the air, and a low shout behind him. For a brief moment he didn't understand what he was seeing. The owl had flown from the tree and grabbed hold of Kaye's head with its talons. Now the bird was flapping and fluttering with both wings extended, a reach that was easily as long as the height of a human being. Feathers, pieces of wood wool, and drops of blood spattered the walls and floor. Kaye was pulling at the owl's legs and body, but it didn't help.

There must have been a lot of sound, but it had momentarily faded. Instead, everything he saw stood out with bright clarity and time slowed down. He crossed the small space to the owl, took hold of the dark, scale-covered legs with one hand and Kaye's head with the other to separate them. But the owl didn't budge, its claws deep in his lover's flesh. In the chaos of blood and hair and feathers he couldn't see if the owl was clasping Kaye's eyes, which was what he feared the most. He pulled at the owl's legs once more, but its shape was so different from anything else he had trained on, he didn't know what to do. How did he force a wild animal to let go of its prey? Spray it with water, yell at it, punch it? Kaye shouted something about not hurting the owl.

He pulled harder and managed to get a single talon loose, but the owl pecked his hand and he reflexively let go of the leg. Now Kaye's face and shirt front were drenched in blood. Head injuries bled a lot, but how much more damage could Kaye take? He took hold of the owl's head, managed somehow to keep the snapping beak away, and put the other hand around the bird's neck. The animal stiffened and shrieked, as if it recognized the death grip. He twisted hard until the vertebrae came loose, like bolts unfastening in their nuts. The owl gaped and shuddered a few times, ejected a stinking mass from its cloacal opening, before it finally, spasmodically, fell away from Kaye.

There was no specific moment when the owl's life ceased, just a slackening of the flesh and a cessation of the will and motion that had previously animated the flesh. Death was uncomplicated that way.

Kaye was clutching his head, blood seeping out between his fingers. He helped Kaye lie down and placed him in a recovery position. "I'll call for an ambulance," he said.

"On the wall," Kaye muttered, beneath what looked like a mask of blood and clumps of curly hair.

The phone had the number for the emergency room of the university hospital written on the cradle in bold marker. He dialed it and gave the emergency team the directions to the institute and the door codes. The hospital was just a few buildings away on campus.

"We'll be there immediately," the person at the other end said. "Stay on the line and we will continue to assist you."

"I can't," he said. "The patient's in another room."

"Do you know any first aid?"

"Yes," he said. "I'll help him and wait for you there."

Without waiting for the reply he tore open the first aid kit by the emergency shower and took all the dressings and compress pads he could find.

When he returned to the sound chamber, Kaye was still bleeding, but breathing. He began to stanch the assistant professor's wounds. Kaye had managed to protect his eyes, but his scalp and hands had deep cuts, soaked in red.

Kaye opened his eyes, the gaze weak and distant, and started struggling to sit up.

"Don't," he said and put a hand on Kaye's chest. "Lie still, the ambulance is on its way." He didn't want Kaye to see all the blood. "How do you feel?" he said, to distract the assistant professor from looking around.

"You killed the owl," Kaye groaned.

"I had to," he said. "It wouldn't let go." He pulled down the zipper of his coverall, stepped out of it, and put it over Kaye. It was flimsy, but better than nothing and would cover some of the blood.

"You killed the owl," Kaye muttered beneath him.

Since he wasn't next of kin he couldn't accompany Kaye in the ambulance, but the emergency personnel gave him a number to call and a floor on the university hospital to go to. He returned to the mouse room and washed his hands in the circular sink with liquid soap from the dispenser, glad the faucet had an optic sensor so there were no handles to sully. Afterward he pushed the faucet from side to side to rinse all the blood away and pulled out a generous amount of paper towels. He dried his hands, then the surface around the sink, clunked the garbage bin beneath it open, and tossed the moist paper in.

On the phone list by the door was a name he recognized:

Narayan, one of Kaye's post-doctoral fellows, and a senior one as far as he had understood from Kaye's stories about his post-docs and graduate students. He pulled out more paper from the dispenser, moistened it with cold water, and wiped the blood off the phone and cradle. Then he dialed the post-doc's number from the list.

"Narayan speaking," a male voice said.

"I'm sorry to call so late," he said, "but professor Kaye's been in an accident in the owl room. No need to worry, he's been taken to the hospital, but there's a bit of a mess here."

"What happened?"

"One of the owls attacked during an experiment."

"How is Kaye? And how's the owl?"

"I think the professor will be all right," he said. "At least he's in good hands now. The owl... didn't make it."

"I see," Narayan said. "Are you a new graduate student or...?"

"I'm the faculty photographer, I've been taking pictures of the owls with Kaye."

"Right," Narayan said. "Kaye mentioned that. I, God, what a shock, who'd think an owl would actually..."

"I should leave for the hospital," he said. "The owl is still here."

"I'll be there right away," Narayan said. "Can you let me know what floor Kaye's in when you get to the hospital?"

"I will," he said. "Thanks so much."

He left the camera bag where it was, perfectly safe behind two coded doors, noted Narayan's number on his phone, fetched his coat in the cloakroom, and rode the elevator down to the first floor. The brightly lit interior made him feel like he was sleepwalking or inside a dream. He suddenly realized that his shirt was full of ominous stains and removed it, then inspected his t-shirt and pants, front and back, in the mirrored walls while he avoided looking at his own face. He rolled the bloody shirt up and put the coat on instead.

A few months ago the news had repeated footage of a missing university student from a hotel elevator somewhere. The young woman, whose ancestry had been from the eastern continent too, was traveling alone on the western continent, where she lived. She had checked into a low-rent hotel which, probably unknown to her, had a history of suspicious deaths. The video from the elevator was the last anyone had seen of the young woman. Via the closed circuit camera some of the last moments of her life were broadcast and watched by millions of people, but only after she was gone, after she had moved past the reach of everyone else, out of the lit circle of safety afforded by civilization and togetherness, and into the darkness beyond. Weeks later the young woman's corpse was found floating in the hotel's water tank on the roof after guests complained that the water "tasted funny."

In the elevator the young woman had pressed several buttons before she leaned out the door to peek into the corridor, as if she were checking to see if there was someone or something following her. She returned inside, squatted in a corner, and pressed all the buttons on the control panel. To him it had looked like she couldn't see the numbers on the elevator buttons properly and had to bend forward to read them. In the photos released to the press the woman wore red square-rimmed glasses, but in the elevator she had used none. If her eyesight was that poor, why had she been in the elevator without her glasses? After the young woman's body was found her death was pronounced an accident, because there was no evidence that other people had accompanied her to the roof.

He was certain the university elevator had a camera too and imagined how he might look if the clip was ever broadcast, in his moment of confusion and distress, desperately wiping blood stains from his shirt.

Outside, it was dark and quiet. It had stopped drizzling but the fog that had lingered all spring and summer still enveloped the city. The street outside The Institute of Biological Sciences was empty, the lamps shining like distant moons in the mist. He couldn't remember the name of the street and was uncertain any taxi company would know where the building was if he called them to the campus without an address. There were no signs nearby, so he started down the road to the student center. It would still be open and there was usually a taxi or two outside.

The moist air cooled his hands and face. He sniffed his fingers. They smelled of copper and wood wool and animal droppings despite the wash. He hoped he didn't reek as he sometimes had after fighting. The headlights of a truck parked on the pavement were reflected by the tiny droplets suspended in the air. He stared at the vehicle. The logo on its front and sides was displayed in pastel pink, blue, and green, with chocolate-covered wafer cones and red and yellow popsicles dancing around it. As he neared the ice cream truck, it started up a chimy tune and the driver's face appeared in the side window. He shook his head and continued.

The phone rang. He jumped, then exhaled slowly before he pulled the phone out from his coat pocket and took the call.

"What's that sound?" Katsuhiro, his younger brother, said. "Are you out buying ice cream at this time of night?" The tune from the truck was slowly receding, but not fast enough.

His first impulse was to hang up to free the line in case Kaye or the hospital called, but he couldn't do that when he had already answered, so now he had to find a way to finish the chat quickly. "No," he said, concentrating on keeping tension out of his voice. "Not really."

Katsuhiro laughed a little at his curtness, but sounded tenser.

"I was just calling to invite you over on Friday night, for beer and snacks. We're testing a new game and have to report any bugs we find, but it's polished beta code so it should be running smoothly. It's beautiful, the areas are so big and there's so much to do, great story, fantastic graphics, it'll be fun, not work."

Seeing Katsuhiro and his friends on the weekend was the last thing he wanted. He had all the reasons in the world to decline, but none that could be shared, and a no would have to be followed up with an excuse that at least sounded genuine. He tried, but couldn't get any white lie going, his mind too busy sorting through the recent events.

"Yes?" he began, hoping that last-second pressure would jog his mind into action. "Why not?" Nothing. He clenched the phone till it creaked.

When they had been ten and twelve, Katsuhiro had once told him: "We have to like the same things because we're brothers."

"Of course we don't," he had said, to Katsuhiro's loud and tearful sorrow. After that it seemed they diverged in most things, especially in relation to their father's culture. He found he enjoyed its traditional performing arts, architecture, and crafts, although he felt distant from it. Katsuhiro, on the other hand, preferred the country's widespread popular culture of games, animation, and movies, and spent years learning the language properly and later found work as a translator for computer games and films. He had always been impressed by Katsuhiro's cultural flexibility while he himself avoided family vacations to both their father's and their mother's country as early as he could. First under the guise of participating in various sports tournaments, later to house sit, take summer classes, or work. Only as adults had Katsuhiro and he found a common ground, which they shared in brief and irregular bursts.

When his brother finally hung up and he could put the phone back in the coat, his hand was sore and imprinted with the phone's corners.

At the university hospital he couldn't face the mirrored enclosure of yet another elevator, and definitely not one with other people in it, so he took the concrete stairwell, ascending it two steps at a time. As he stood panting in the corridor of the floor Kaye had been brought to, a nurse told him that the assistant professor's wounds had been disinfected, stitched, and dressed, the patient given a tetanus shot and antibiotics, and sent home.

"Did you really discharge him?" he said. "He lost a lot of blood."

"The patient was young and healthy and we only do blood transfusions when it's absolutely necessary," the nurse said, giving him a pointed look.

He nodded. "I hope the patient didn't leave all by himself?"

"No, someone came and picked him up," the nurse said. "Don't worry, I'm certain your friend made it home safely."

"Thank you," he said.

He exited the hospital's main entrance and headed for the bus stop across the street. On the way there and while waiting for the bus he almost called Kaye twice. Instead, he texted Narayan on the bus home, rested his hands in his lap, and closed his eyes against the glare of the lamps in the ceiling.

At the honeycomb towers, Michael had let himself into the apartment, made dinner for them both, and eaten.

"Sorry I'm so late," he said, removing his shoes and hanging up his jacket by the front door. "The professor I've been working for had to go to the hospital."

"Is he all right?" Michael said. "What happened?"

He rubbed his face. He felt terrible. "One of the owls attacked him. I guess something must have frightened it." He went into the bathroom and turned on the faucet.

Michael was a quiet shadow in the doorway. "What about you then, are you all right?"

"Yes," he said, "just need to clean up a little." He turned on the tap and washed his hands thoroughly before wiping his face and neck with cool water. "Thank you," he said, "for making food, and for waiting." Michael leaned over and hugged him.

Yet later, when Michael was a warm silhouette next to him in the muted shine from the bedroom window, the image of Kaye's face being torn into by the owl's talons played over and over in his mind and he wanted to leave the bed, pull the clothes back on as quickly as he could, and run out the door. But then he remembered he was at home, so instead he forced himself to lie still and sweat among the sheets while he listened to Michael sleep inside the stuffy darkness.

The next morning he caught a bus to the old part of the city and walked the short distance from the stop to Kaye's house. The windows were dark and it was quiet. The mist beaded the smooth triangular leaves that covered the trunk and branches of the monkey puzzle tree like plate mail, the droplets catching the gray light. The air smelled of earth and rain, with an undertone of rot. He pressed the doorbell, heard it ring inside, and waited. If Kaye was in bed, which the professor ought to, it would take time for him to reach the door. He hoped Kaye instead would open the lower right panel in the bedroom window and drop the keys to him, as on earlier occasions. But there were no steps in the stairs, no creaking on the floor behind the door, no window pane that opened. He rang the doorbell once more. Perhaps Kaye was asleep? Maybe he should have called before he arrived? A third ring only brought more silence.

He turned and started on the brief walk back to the bus stop while he dialed Kaye's number.

"Please leave a message after the tone."

He called Narayan instead. "Have you seen Kaye today?" he

said after he introduced himself. His cheeks and hands were moist from the fog.

"I haven't," Narayan said. "I assume he's at home taking care of himself. At least he should be."

"How did the owl room look?"

"Awful. I called the university's cleaning service, but all that blood seemed dangerous so I wiped up a little first, and threw it in the biohazard bin before they arrived. But everything is clean now."

"What about the owl?"

"I put it in the freezer for dissection later on. Who knows, the bird might have been sick, injured, or had some kind of parasite, which caused the sudden change in behavior."

He nodded. "Let me know if there is anything I can help with."

"Not much we can do about the owl now," Narayan said. "But better it than professor Kaye. How badly was he hurt?"

"I didn't see the wounds clearly, they had to be cleaned first," he said. "But I'm certain the owl missed Kaye's eyes. He wouldn't have been sent home so quickly if not."

"Good point. It can't have been that serious then."

"I left the camera bag in the owl room, but will pick it up as soon as I can. If Kaye calls tonight, will you let him know I said hello?"

"Of course."

He downloaded, prepared, and sent the last batch of photos to Kaye's email account. Then he sent the professor a text message wishing him a good and speedy recovery. He didn't stop by Kaye's house, thinking that the professor needed sleep to heal. Instead he went home to the honeycomb towers.

He texted Michael, but there was no reply. Maybe Michael was still at work, preparing mathematical simulations of financial risk that were going to run the whole night. He showered and pulled on the terrycloth bathrobe and slippers he had pilfered from some hotel abroad, padded out to the elevator, and upstairs to the swimming pool. At the time of planning, a pool on the top floor probably seemed like a good idea to draw more buyers to the overpriced apartments instead of a few large and even more difficult to sell penthouses, but now, with the towers built and populated, not many inhabitants seemed to have the time or the inclination to use the large space and water.

As usual at night, the cold unlit room beneath the vaulted glass ceiling was empty, and the water's surface still. He stepped out of his slippers and left the bathrobe on one of the white plastic chairs furthest away from the pool so it wouldn't get wet. Then he dove in and swam two laps, fifty meters, under water, with slow, deliberate motions, finishing each arm stroke before starting on the leg stroke. When that was done he crawled fifty laps on the surface, quietly, in the darkness. Afterward, he floated in the water for a long time while he watched the cloud of stars at the center of the galaxy rise above the silhouette of the marsh and the city center in the distance, feeling like every shining point of light moved and lived inside him.

"Sometimes when I think about you, it's like there's nobody there," Kaye once told him. They were lying in the broad bed on the second floor of Kaye's house. As the dining room downstairs, the bedroom was filled with antique furniture in a ruddy wood with carved legs and miniature pilasters: the stout double bed, a two-door closet with matte elliptical mirrors, and two bedside tables. Paperbacks, hardbound, and jacketed books, mixed with academic journals and photo prints were stacked in a blast radius around the bed.

"I'm here," he said. "I always am."

10

HE DIDN'T RECEIVE ANY MORE REQUESTS FOR photographic assignments from the faculty, but nevertheless sent them his resignation letter, preferring to believe that he had preemptively quit, rather than been fired.

Beanie, Michael's sister, came over. At first she was yelling a stream of unflattering descriptions because she had recently thrown her boyfriend out, despite not being able to pay the rent on the apartment they shared on her own. But as her anger cooled it turned to tears.

"It's so unfair!" Beanie said, crumpling the tissue paper he had offered her against the crying, and which she had wept and blown her nose into several times, and threw it against the living room wall. "Just because he's a cheating bastard, I have to move out! I love that apartment! I found it!"

He wanted to go and pick up the moist wad and place it in the bin in the bathroom, but instead he said, "Why don't you come and stay here?"

"And live with you?" Beanie said, but then lowered her head and voice. "This apartment is too small for two people."

That was the argument Michael had used when he'd suggested

they move in together, more than a year ago. "No, I just need a house sitter," he said.

Beanie pulled another tissue from the plastic pack in her lap and wiped her cheeks. "Thank you," she said, "but I can't afford it. Freelance music producers don't earn that much."

"I'd rather have someone I know stay here instead of renting it to strangers," he said. "I could pay part of the cost if you wanted to stay and look after the cats."

Beanie lit up so much he regretted not having mentioned it sooner. "Would you really do that?"

He nodded.

"For how long?"

"A few months," he said. "Maybe half a year."

She frowned. "Where are you going?"

"Work."

"Did you sign up again?" Beanie looked as if she had been waiting for it, that she thought he was stupid enough to do that.

"No," he huffed. "It's not like that."

"Thank goodness," Beanie said, her relief as touching as it was annoying. She looked at him. "Does Michael know?"

"I'll tell him soon," he said.

"You must."

"I will. I promise."

Beanie stood. "All right," she said. "I'll start packing right away."

"But no smoking," he said. She wasn't allowed to when she was visiting.

Beanie sighed, then bulged her upper lip with her tongue at him to emulate the small packets of ground and moistened tobacco that had become increasingly popular, even among women, as smoking became less and less accepted. "I'll have to start snuffing then," she said.

He made steak and a green leaf salad for dinner, no rice nor pasta, and a shake of blueberries, lemongrass, and spirulina for dessert for Michael and himself. After the meal they watched the news together: floods to the north, crop failures on the eastern continent, hurricanes on the western continent, drought on the entire southern continent, food prices going up all over the world, demonstrations, riots, wars.

"I thank the gods every day that we live in a place that is peaceful and has few natural disasters," Michael said.

When the news was finished, he brought the laptop over to the sofa and showed the image on the screen to Michael.

"I've found a cabin," he said.

Michael leaned past him for a closer look. The red one-story structure had been photographed from the air. The nearby hillock wasn't tall enough to put the cabin in shade and in the far distance a lake glittered under the blue sky, making the area look generous and sunny. The cabin's sharply gabled roof was dark with solar cell panels and the deck in the front was unpainted, but tidy.

"There'll be lots of mosquitoes with all those trees nearby," Michael said and started scrolling down the website to the realtor's information about the property. "How old is this thing anyway?"

"Just a decade," he replied. "But it's built from re-used wood. It was the previous owner's pet project."

"'Has its own well and solar cell panels, no municipal water supply or electricity,'" Michael read. "That's certainly basic. Are you sure the previous owner didn't die from a heart attack while cutting firewood or pumping water from the well?"

"No," he said, "she died at home from old age."

"So the previous owner is dead," Michael said. "And how on Earth do you know that?"

"I phoned the realtor," he said.

"You're serious about this?"

He nodded.

"Are you leaving?" Michael said. "Without me?"

"That's why I'm showing you the cabin," he said. "Come with me."

"For how long?" Michael said, frowning.

"I don't know," he said. "For as long as necessary."

Michael sighed and looked at him as if he were a beloved, but naughty puppy who had just peed in his favorite shoes.

"I can't," Michael finally said. "I have my family, my friends, my job here. And what are you going to do up there anyway?"

"Renovate the cabin?" he said, but it came out much less certain than he had intended.

Michael gave him the look again. "You've already bought the place, haven't you?"

He nodded.

When he was a toddler his mother took him to a nearby park that had a large circular fountain on its thin lawn. The fountain's shallow but wide basin was bounded by a simple concrete ring. The fountainhead in the middle was dry and had rusted shut a long time ago, leaving the water smooth and dark. He enjoyed sitting on the circumference while stirring the lukewarm, algae-green water and watching the reflections caught in its surface. As the mirror images of the knobby trunks and leafless branches of the brutally sheared oaks behind the pool trembled and merged into one other, the sound of the surrounding children and their guardians muted to nothing. Even from far away the fountain blinked like an eye between the streets and houses.

When his parents found a new home in another neighborhood they stopped going to the park and he forgot about the fountain, until his teens, when he started seeing a round body of water the color of the sky in his dreams. As an adult he once passed through the park by coincidence. Recognizing the foot-path that led up to the fountain, he began to hurry, eager to see if the eye of water was really there at the top of the hill, as it always was in his dreams, or whether it was just something he had made up. He ran the last stretch, expecting to see only brown grass and bushes shivering in the cold spring gale, but when he reached the top of the slope, the fountain was there, its encompassing basin shallower and more algae-filled than before, the flagstones littered with gravel from the winter's ice and snow, and the oaks grown taller and thicker than he remembered them. He marveled at having found the place from his childhood that he still visited in his dreams, and sat by the pool for a long time, watching the reflections of the bleak clouds rush across the sky in the water. Having revisited the site in his waking life, he never saw the fountain again in his dreams.

The train line from the honeycomb towers was closed due to a power failure in the grid, so he had to take a bus to the central station for the journey to the mountains and the cabin. On the way there the street filled with people: women, men, young, middle-aged, elderly, who carried posters and banners, shouted slogans and sang, and banged on the windows of the bus and the other vehicles that came to a halt. The crowd was protesting against the city council's increased taxes and the cost of utilities such as water, power, and renovation. The bus driver pulled into a side street to get away from the demonstration, but even there the traffic was choked by people.

After half an hour with barely any movement, the passengers became restless. First, a man in a suit and tie rose from his seat and told the bus driver to open the door to let him out on the narrow pavement. The man exited and was swallowed by the crowd. Fifteen minutes later a young couple in fleece jackets and large backpacks exited the bus too. The traffic remained still for a while longer, then started and stopped a few times, like a vehicle with ignition trouble, before it flowed again. But because of the detour and the unfamiliar streets he couldn't tell if they were getting nearer or further away from the station. The small TV screens above the seats were filled with news images of buildings on fire, vessels spilling refugees in a stormy sea, livestock carcasses drying in parched fields, canoes navigating flooded suburban gardens. Then they showed another demonstration, in another city, on another continent, it wasn't clear which, maybe from several different places, not just one. He took in the images of the political manifestations on TV, and marveled at how it was mirrored by the shouting crowd that surrounded the bus, before he turned his gaze back to the throng on the screens.

11

THE WATER IN THE OLD POT HAD BEGUN TO BOIL, convection bubbles bursting on the surface of the liquid. He reached for the handle to move the pot off the flame, but a brightness flared inside him and flooded his mind. He was familiar with the brightness; it was nothing new. He had first seen it in his sleep when he was little. At that time it caused nothing more than slightly painful contractions along his spine. During the previous spring the brightness became impossible to ignore, but he had gradually grown used to it. After the initial blast it usually faded to a glow behind his thoughts, but now, in the solitude of the cabin with nothing to distract him, the brightness overtook him. He was distantly aware that his legs buckled beneath him and that he banged against the stove, faintly hoping that he wouldn't knock the boiling water over and glad he had placed it on a ring in the back. Then the light outshone everything else. Inside it, he was what he had been before he was born and what he would become when his body was forgotten.

The multi-colored rug was accordioned beneath his hips and against the canister beneath the stove. He blinked and reached for the knobs above him, thinking he could at least turn the flame off, but fell into the light again like a drowning person sliding back into water.

The second time the world came into view he fumbled hard against the front of the stove and almost managed to reach the knob. If he had been home his two cats would have found him and curled up against him, unaware of his struggle. Instead, he heard a tapping on the glass above him and wondered if it had started to rain.

A face, round and pale like the moon, was staring in through the pane in the door. He was half beneath it, half up against the stove, and too close to be fully seen from the outside. The water on the stove hissed and spat tiny needles, which occasionally landed on his skin. The neighbor knocked on the window again.

"Are you all right?" the face asked, breath misting the old glass, voice muted by the barrier. Was that Mark? "If you move a little, I can open the door and come inside!"

"I'm fine, thank you!" he shouted and wriggled closer to the door. "Don't worry!"

"Are you sure?"

"Yes, of course."

At university he had an acquaintance, a pre-med student, who used to tell a story of how she saved one of her neighboring students when he suffered a seizure while frying ground beef to mix with pasta.

"I heard an odd shout and then there was a bang against the wall," the pre-med student would say. "I recognized the yell as that of an epileptic fit, dropped everything I had, and ran into my neighbor's room. He was indeed having a seizure, didn't even know he had epilepsy. I saved him," she said, again and again. Every time the pre-med told the story he made a mental note to stay silent if he ever had a fit.

"Eloise and I bought some rice that was on sale in the store," Mark said. "We bought a bag for you too, if you want it. Have to take advantage of a sale, especially since the prices have jumped again. I'll just put the bag here." There was a thud on the deck and something fell against the door.

"Thank you so much!" he said, guilt blossoming up inside him for keeping Mark out while the neighbor was only being friendly. "How much was it?"

"Oh, please don't worry about it," Mark said. "It was on sale."

"No, no," he said. "Please let me pay for it."

"It's nothing, we're neighbors, after all," Mark said. "Consider it a house-warming gift."

"Thank you!" he shouted. "That's too kind of you. Would you like to come in for some tea?" He wasn't certain if he would be able to make any tea, but felt he had to offer.

"Thanks, I'm fine," Mark said. "I have to hurry, Eloise and the children are waiting for me in the car. Take care now!"

He managed to roll over, the bunched-up rug following his movements. Now he faced the ceiling, with the front of the stove rearing over him like a gawking passerby. From there he reached up, curled his fingers around the knob and got just enough leverage to twist it around to zero. The hiss from the nearly invisible blue flame that billowed around the ring in the back and the spattering from the pot faded. He leaned into the rug, its folds smelling of dust and mold. Then the white light caught up with him and he made certain not to make any strange or loud sounds.

12

IN HIS DREAMS IT WAS PAST MIDNIGHT, BUT STILL not dark, with a golden shine behind the round mountains in the distance. The night was soft and mild, and soon sparrows would wake and sing. On the ground, crocus flowers shone violet, petals beady with dew, cupping their orange stamen. There was a breath of wind, like the touch from a hand, then the warmth of the pre-dawn landscape enveloped him again.

The crocus pickers whispered to one another as they worked, smiling, laughing quietly. Their diaphanous robes fluttered in the air, indigo and purple hemmed with gold. They deposited their harvest on a carpet of woven silk in the middle of the field, for quick fingers to peel the thin petals and gain the stamens that shivered inside.

At the edges of the meadow the crocus pickers' children were tended to by siblings or elderly relatives. As he watched, the children grew old enough to participate in the work and joined their families on the flower field. A little while longer and those children had conceived children of their own, who also accompanied their parents to the meadow, and with time replaced them. In the stream that flowed past the meadow, the water gilt with predawn light, a heron lifted, spreading rings upon the surface.

He woke, thinking about Eloise and Mark and their reasons for initiating the project.

In the morning the head of the space organization's program for manned exploration was interviewed on TV about the astronaut selection process. He watched it on the laptop using his phone as modem. Even here the network was fast enough to stream broadcast and video.

"But is it right to spend all this money, technology, and brain power on sending people into space instead of feeding the billions who are starving, or giving the displaced new livelihoods and housing?" the TV host, a woman in her mid-fifties with brown hair cut in a thick bob, an ivory-colored silk blouse, and a large enamel necklace of daisies, asked.

He scoffed, doubting that the TV host had experienced much hunger or displacement herself.

The head of the space organization, a slim, middle-aged, salt-and-pepper-haired man in a dark suit, leaned close to the host, and winked. "Well, you know, we're a lot cheaper to run than the defense program."

The TV host smiled.

"We must of course reduce the hunger and poverty in the world, and help all those who have lost their homes in recent disasters, but the technology and discoveries from space find multiple uses in industry and innovation world-wide. The missions we have planned will benefit all people on Earth," the head of the space organization concluded, and looked like he meant it.

13

ONCE THE NEIGHBORS STARTED ON THE TASK,
they cleared the heather in a few weeks. Their heavy machinery rumbled and grated even through the night, with the beams
from the vehicles' headlights passing over the panorama window in the cabin like curious glances. When it was dark outside
he averted his eyes from the farmers' noisy illumination, and
during the day he avoided looking at the abrupt changes they
had effected on the moor. He regretted having allowed them
to clear and plough the land around the cabin, but Mark and
Eloise's fields were so close, the razing would have been visible
whether he had granted them permission or not.

As the heath grew increasingly brown and cultivated, his
refusal to look at it mounted. If he didn't see the moor while it
was being cleared, but instead only looked at it again once it had
become fully domesticated, the change might feel less abrupt.
But after avoiding the heath for several days, one morning he
had to see the newly born farmland for himself. He pulled on
his running pants, t-shirt, and socks he hadn't laundered in the
kitchen sink yet, and his trainers. When he finally stood on the
deck, the breeze was cold but the sun warmed his back. The
sky was crisp and clear, the mountains below it the dark color

of the ocean in the fall. The moor smelled of overturned earth and grass, as if spring had skipped winter and arrived early. He couldn't remember the last time the sky had been clear in the city, and was glad he had relocated.

Before the cabin the exposed soil stretched brown and bare, only interrupted here and there by gray stones that resembled pale, hairless pates peeking up from the dirt. There were no paths or roads along the fields, so he decided to run across them. The route would be a few kilometers at least and give him a closer look at what the farmers had done. He breathed and yawned, stretched his arms, back, and legs. Then he stepped out onto the soft, wet soil. The trainers sank into the ground. The shoes would need a good rinse afterward, but it would be worth it. Besides, he had to be in shape in case he progressed in the astronaut selection. The yielding substrate would make it more difficult to keep his balance, and would slow him down, but it would also add to the exercise.

He began by walking briskly to get warm, before he stretched again at a cluster of slim birches on an unplowed mound a few hundred meters from the cabin. With the shortening of the days, the birches had turned yellow, which looked odd in the spring-like morning. The breeze nevertheless chilled his face and cleared his mind and he was glad he had decided to face the fields. He started running and focused on maintaining his balance in the soft soil to avoid sprains. Keeping a moderate pace, he passed the grooves and furrows Eloise and Mark's machinery had created in the sea of brown. He ran in the direction his eyes usually traced behind the panorama window in the cabin, from south to north along the blue mountains. It felt good to finally follow that path with the rest of his body.

When the cabin had become small behind him, he turned and ran parallel with the fields. Mark and Eloise had mentioned barley, rye, even winter wheat. He imagined the heath ripe with tall, whispering grain. Would those crops really grow here? How did the farmers know the wheat would survive? What if the cold winters returned, or became even harsher, or the weather changed in some other, unexpected way? It was a risk, one the neighbors seemed eager, even desperate to take. He realized the documents Mark and Eloise had given him didn't describe how the project was financed or how much it would cost. He had spotted in the papers the green and white logo of the bank in the town center, so he assumed they were involved. Eloise had also mentioned funding from the department of agriculture at the local university. The documentation included long-term climate models from the meteorological service and soil and mineral analyses from the national geological survey. But he doubted those institutions funded any external projects. He intended to ask Eloise and Mark about it, although it wouldn't change anything. The investment had already been done, the financial gambit made. With the news reporting soaring food prices and shrinking crops on all continents, the project made sense, even good sense. But he nevertheless felt unsettled about it, like a warning he had received and then forgotten, the shadow of a Kraken passing beneath the surface.

His concerns about the project made him forget his surroundings until his thoughts shone in a lightless void, where there was no him or body or field or sky, only the thoughts standing sharply out from the silence that surrounded them. In the warm darkness something gleamed, like a spinning coin. When he became aware of it, the brightness rushed forward and engulfed him, like it had in the kitchen earlier.

The Hercules-Corona Borealis Great Wall had been discovered because of the extremely powerful gamma ray bursts that shot out from it and reached the Earth after millions of years. He had once watched an animation about how gamma ray bursts were created, how they surged forth from the center of a super-nova as it imploded when the giant star's multiple layers of pure elements collapsed in on each other. The unimaginably strong beam of energy ripped itself from the core of the star, jetting as close to the speed of light as it was possible to come. On the way the ray plumed outward like water from a fountainhead or the tip of a bullet blooming on impact, before it narrowed into a beam that pierced the surface at both ends of the now dead star and shot out as gigantic, swirling rays of pure gamma radiation.

"These explosions are so powerful," the narrator of the video said, "that they are visible from the other side of the universe."

Now it felt like a gamma ray burst went off inside him, exploding him in luminance, filling him, then jetting out his eyes and ears and mouth. Social inhibition and self-consciousness forgotten, he emitted a low shout and pitched into the soil. He couldn't feel his body hit the ground, only that cold mud started seeping through his t-shirt and pants. When he tried to get up, he only became more soaked. Then all he knew was the supernova light.

The sun was vanishing. Since his back and side were drenched, it grew chilly. He registered the fading light and cooling temperature, but when he lifted his head and hands to get up, the gamma ray burst surged and pulled him down again.

The next time his eyes fluttered open one side of him was comfortable, while the other was cold. But the warmth that was there made the chill bearable and he thought he might not freeze to death after all. The sun had long since crept behind the mountains, yet the dusk was almost as blue and soft as it had been in the city in the summer. A wall of eyes were watching him, black, shiny orbs above short, stout beaks, belonging to small feathered bodies. He blinked. He must be dreaming. A flock of white and brown sparrows were sitting on his chest and belly and limbs, covering him like a blanket. There must be at least a hundred of them, if not a hundred and fifty. When he lifted his head to look more closely at the birds they didn't fly away as he thought they would, but rocked and swayed with his motions while they clutched his clothes and skin and calmly took him in.

Then the gray shingles and the black plastic gutter that edged the roof of the cabin were angled above him. He smelled like he did after he had killed Kaye's owl, the earthy, coppery fragrance of unconcealed perspiration and sudden, violent death.

"How lucky we found you," someone said nearby. A face he recognized as one of his neighbors was looking down at him, together with several others. He searched for Eloise and Mark, but they were not there.

"And lucky we hadn't started manuring the fields yet," another neighbor said and laughed.

14

"WE SAW A LARGE FLOCK OF SPARROWS BANK IN the air and had to go see what it was," the neighbor closest to him said, whose name he couldn't recall.

"You thought it might be someone trying to beat us to the sowing," another one said.

"Shush," the first neighbor replied.

"When we got closer the birds took to the air and then we saw you on the ground."

"We thought you were dead!"

"Shhh!"

He looked at them. "Thank you for the help," he said.

"Are you all right? Do you need help to get inside?"

"No," he said. "I need to rinse off first."

"You probably shouldn't lie on the ground this time of year, it's too cold."

"And definitely not after we've sown or when the crops have started to grow!"

They helped him up, said goodbye, then retreated to the path that wound past the cabin and down to Mark and Eloise's farm. Now he saw they were all wearing tall rubber boots and fluorescent-colored vests, and that one of them had what in the moonlit darkness looked like the barrel of a shotgun hanging over her arm. The neighbors mounted two four-wheeled motorbikes and drove off in a spray of sludge and soil and noise, leaving a deep hush behind them.

He stood, switched on the six-sided glass lantern in the corner of the deck's railing. The solar-powered light flickered a little, then cast a weak yet steady shine over the mud-dappled planks. Almost immediately the flitting shadows of mosquitoes and other flying insects appeared in the corona from the lamp.

He was shivering so hard it was difficult to stand upright and he had to clench his jaws to keep them from clattering. He peered down his torso, passed his quivering hands over his ears and neck and throat, and stretched his tensed limbs to look for ticks and other pests that may have attached themselves from the soil. From his memory the scent of sand and sun lotion appeared, from days on the beach by the artificial lake in the city when he ignored his mother's calls from the shore, staying in the water until his lips were purple and his body shook.

He smiled at the recollection, shuffled over to the tap on the wall and pushed one end of the rubber hose that lay coiled beneath it onto the spigot. Then he attached the other end to the shower head that hung on a hook high above the tap. When he stepped into the spray the water was so cold it made him gasp and intensified his shivering. He rinsed his hair and skin as well as the shaking allowed, turned the faucet off, and hurried inside, leaving his muddied trainers, running pants, and underwear like shed skin on the deck.

He was shaking too hard to light the firewood in the hearth. Instead he pulled all his clothes out of the backpack until he found the beach towel he had brought from the city. When his skin was dry and his hair dripping less, he wrapped the metal foil emergency blanket from his first aid kit around himself and curled up in the sleeping bag, pulling its broad top over his head. There, he shivered for hours until he fell asleep without noticing.

The next morning he went outside in the cold sunlight to rinse the clothes on the deck in the improvised shower and hang them to dry over the banister. Inside he rolled the clothes he had pulled out up again and stuffed them into the backpack. Then he found Eloise and Mark's phone number in the project folder and invited them over.

This time, when Mark and Eloise arrived with the other neighbors and squashed together on the sofa, he had clean cups and teaspoons, hot tea, and a bowl with lumps of refined sugar waiting for them.

"I thought you only fertilized in the spring," he said when the small talk was out of the way.

"Usually," Eloise said. "But the soil is so virgin we thought we'd give it a boost by fertilizing it lightly and turn it once more before the frost, to prepare it for the spring."

"You must till the land again then?" he said.

"Yes," Mark said, "because there's always frost in the winter, even if it doesn't snow."

"Does it snow much here?"

"Lots, or it used to. Now we're lucky if we have a week of white in the winter."

"It's made the animals confused, bears come out of their dens in January and butterflies start swarming in March. The rabbits have almost disappeared because their white coat now gives them away instead of camouflaging them."

"You snared several mottled rabbits last December, didn't you?"

The neighbor who had done this nodded. "They looked like they didn't know whether it was winter or spring."

"Do you really think wheat will grow here?" he said. "At this latitude and elevation?"

The tea cups clinked, lowered almost simultaneously.

"Haven't you read the papers?" Eloise said. "We had meteorologists at the local university compare the temperatures of the past decades with the newest projections from climate scientists and plant experts, proper research, mind you. We even received a grant from the ministry for agriculture as a special project."

So that's where the funding for the seeds and the fertilizer and the four-wheeled motorbikes came from. He looked at them. "And you also made personal investments into this?"

"Where did you hear that?"

"It's a small town," he lied. It was worth a try, there had to be lots of gossip around about the project.

Mark nodded. "Most of us have put our savings into it, we refinanced our farm. We'll be all right."

"Well worth the labor to get away from lumber and wood pulp production if you ask me," Eloise said. "Those are no longer viable."

"No pain, no gain?" he said.

"No risk, no gain," Eloise replied. "Those who are not too risk adverse may find the changes in weather profitable and opening up new possibilities. And why not, it's our moor, our land."

He nodded and looked down into his tea. "But what if the weather changes again?"

"How? And to what?" Eloise nearly yelled.

15

HE DREAMED HE WAS GIVEN A KNIFE FROM HIS
father's country, a traditionally crafted dagger with the short
handle wrapped tightly in ordered loops of black cotton, the
bronze silhouette of a dragon spiraling among clouds secured
inside it. The knife's guard was a thin disc of steel with an intri-
cate, curling pattern of negative space.

He took the knife with his right hand, held it horizontally, and
with the left hand pulled back the lacquered wooden sheath. The
steel in the single-edged blade had tiny particles that sparkled like
sunlight on snow, or the galaxy clusters in the Hercules-Corona
Borealis Great Wall, so luminous he had to squint against them,
even inside the dream.

At first, he was enthralled by the beauty of the knife and the
ancient craftsmanship with which it had been made, but then
he realized it had been made for killing, to assassinate someone
specific, and that knowledge hit him like a punch to the gut.

He woke up regretting what he had done the past months, getting involved with Kaye, killing the owl, leaving Michael and
his family, buying the cabin, being pulled into the neighbors'
agrarian project. The remorse sat like lead in his bones. Other

thoughts rushed past like water around a boulder in a river. He was anchored by regret, everything else was fluid.

In his inbox was a note from the space organization. His application to the astronaut training program had made it out of the initial round and the organization required more information and tests. Attached to the mail was the medical form for a private piloting license, necessary for the second round of selection. He needed a physician to do a general examination and the electrocardiogram test that was required for the certificate, plus sign the form which asked if he had any kind of heart or circulatory disease, high blood pressure, asthma, diabetes, and a whole list of other ailments. Previous pilot or scuba diving licenses could be submitted instead, provided they had not been issued more than two years in the past, making his scuba diving license too old to use. He had to find a local physician who would see him and sign the license as soon as possible, otherwise he would have to find a doctor in the city and take the train back. When he realized he might have to return home, he almost grabbed his backpack to start on the hike to the concrete platform where the rail tracks reached into the pine forest in both directions.

Instead, he got up on legs that were asleep from sitting on the floor for too long, limped to the firewood he had stacked in the now completed northwestern corner of the living room and brought two of the logs and a twig with him to the hearth. He placed the logs on the ashes, fetched the lighter from the top drawer in the kitchen, and lit the twig, let it burn a little, before he put the flame to the logs so they caught fire too. The new warmth made him shiver and he moved as close to the hearth as possible and stared into the flames for a long while.

As he had suspected, none of the local physicians listed online were authorized to sign the medical test that the space organization required.

"The closest person who can issue certificates is on the coast," they informed him when he called the doctors' offices, giving him the name of a small town two stops closer on the rail line than his home city. He'd save little more than an hour's travel by going there. But since he didn't trust himself to not give everything up and flee back to Michael and the apartment once he was home, he decided to go to the coast instead. He found the doctor the local physicians had mentioned online, phoned her office, and scheduled an appointment later in the week.

Several hours by train through mountains and valleys covered in red and orange oak, ash, aspen, birch, beech, and rowan, interspersed with green from fir, spruce, juniper, and yew, took him to the coast. On that part of the continent the forest reached almost down to the ocean and just a narrow band of pebble beaches and round-backed islets, many only visible at low tide, kept the sea from the land.

As most other small towns along the coast, it was a holiday resort, and like most such places it went into hibernation in late autumn. Visiting such places out of season was unsettling and alienating, like staying in a large office after everyone else has left. The physical objects, the streets and buildings and shops and piers, were still there, in the same location as they would be in the summer, with even some of the carts that sold hot dogs and ice cream and candy floss, and some of the booths that offered t-shirts and postcards and model ships in the high season, were still open, but the lack of people, the surplus of public space, and the gray light of autumn, made everything look run down and lonely.

Large tracts of the seaside walk were covered in scaffolding and put in dry dock by temporary wooden walls. There, the water had been bilged back into the ocean by peristaltic pipes and compressors, although the enclosures were wet and slowly refilling. Plastic signs bearing the town's crest explained that the seaside walk was in the process of being elevated and strengthened to be able to withstand the increased erosion of the higher sea level and more frequent winter storms. The text further apologized for the unsightly conditions and claimed that the process would be complete by a date several years into the future.

He nevertheless enjoyed the stroll along the sea, the hiss of the white waves against the stone, the constant wind from the ocean, and the dim, heavy sky. The gale nipped at his mountain jacket and he was glad he was carrying his thirty-liter backpack, since it helped keep the wind out. The rain tasted salty from the spray of the waves and he had to stop for a moment to take his leather gloves out of the backpack and pull them on.

On his way along the frothing seaside, he passed a wall so thick with layer upon layer of glued-on posters and flyers the surface seemed almost like papier mache. The announcements advertised the previous summer's performances by various bands, stand-up comedians, tattoo masters, circus acts, fortune tellers, and magicians. He passed his eyes over the rotting, water-peeled sheets to find the most overdone and improbable of them. But then one of the posters presented a familiar name, an address in the town center, and a time just a few hours into the future. Blood shot into his head and he suddenly felt warm. The still-intact paper and the not-yet-faded print hinted that the ad was relatively recent. He gaped, looked again, then took out his phone and photographed the address on the flyer. With his heart beating hard, he continued to the doctor's office.

In a corner of the waiting room stood a small spruce, its flat, shiny needles revealing its plastic nature, decorated with small electrical lights and glittering red tinsel. Lengths of artificial mistletoe garlanded the walls of the room. He smirked a little at the festive display, December being several months away. But here, summer probably started right after Easter and lasted till the autumn holidays. No wonder they wanted Christmas to arrive as quickly as possible.

"You're going for a pilot's license, then?" the doctor, a brown-haired woman just a few years older than him, said as she fastened a blood pressure cuff around his arm.

"Yes, starting this spring," he lied. Trying out for the astronaut selection wasn't something he wished to share, especially not to a stranger.

"That's rare," the doctor said. "I mostly see requests for diving licenses, you know with the tourists and all, but the tests are nearly identical."

He nodded. "I'm tempted to get that license too," he said for the sake of small talk.

The doctor performed all the necessary tests, for blood pressure, heart status, lung function, hearing, ear-nose-throat, visual acuity, and color blindness. He had emailed the form in advance and the doctor promised to fill it out, sign it, and send it back to him within a week.

When he left the doctor's office it had grown almost dark. The rain had ceased, giving way to a rushing wind. At the edge of the horizon, between the black ocean and the pewter sky, a slice of orange burned, like the last embers of a fire. The drawstrings on his jacket whipped in the gale and even inside the gloves his fingers began to feel cold and stiff. He pulled out the schedule he'd picked up at the train station, the paper dog-eared and damp from his pocket. The next train left at six, the last one at nine. It was nearly five o'clock. He decided to attend the meeting advertised by the poster.

Hoping to get away from the worst of the wind, he continued one street inland from the pier, looking for a restaurant or cafe that served dinner early. A little further he saw a flimsy glass front with letters in gold foil announcing that the food served there was eastern, and hurried inside.

Although the place was clearly for take-outs, two small tables with round stools tucked beneath them flanked the door. He nodded at the man behind the counter, who addressed him in an eastern language he didn't understand.

"Sorry," he said in the language of the coastal country they were in. "Are you still serving lunch?"

"Lunch, dinner, whatever you need," the man said, in their common language.

"May I eat here?"

"Of course," the man said. "What do you wish to order?"

He took in the lit posters behind the cook which displayed the variety of dishes the small restaurant offered, and ordered a dinner plate of beef and broccoli with rice. He sat down by the window, pulled the backpack off, removed his jacket, and draped it over the other stool so it would dry a little. The room was chilly and humid, and the air itself felt greasy, dense with the smell of food and cooking oil, which only made him hungrier. He hadn't eaten anything before he left the cabin in the morning. Outside in the gray dusk the streetlamps blinked on one by one, first hesitantly, then burning steadily, and scraps of paper rolled past in the gale.

When the food arrived it turned out to be surprisingly good, the beef cut into tender pieces that had been marinated and fried well, the onion and broccoli glazed and still firm, the rice not too hard and not too soft, just as he preferred it, and sauteed in a dark, strong broth. Crystals of artificial food flavoring crunched between the grains of rice. He knew it wasn't just salt, but since he hadn't had eastern food in a long time, he ate it anyway. He also received a glass of water that tasted of the air in the restaurant, and a cup of sweet, honey-colored tea. He consumed all of the food and when he was done he felt sated, yet not too full.

"Good?" the cook asked. He nodded and pulled out a paper napkin from the steel dispenser on the table and patted his lips.

The cook nodded back at him, then returned to filling an order that was called in by phone.

He checked his messages and email, sent a short text to Beanie wondering how she and the cats were doing. Could he ask how she was treating his apartment or would that sound like he didn't trust her? He'd made her promise not to smoke inside, but he assumed that when she had people over, there was smoking in the apartment, at least on the veranda. He imagined a tray bristling with cigarette butts and ashes, overflowing from rain and weeping stinking water on the concrete.

The cook pointed a remote at a small black screen above the other table and switched to the news: more protests and rallies against public budget cuts, lowered quality of healthcare, dwindling pension funds, increased unemployment. Four vessels filled with migrants had been intercepted at the southern coast of the continent and escorted back to international waters. What would happen with those ships? Would they try again and sink in the attempt as countless others had done before them? Yet another increase in the price of power, gasoline, air travel, and meat. Water shortage and unrest on the eastern continent, forest fires and dust storms on the western continent, drought and famine on the southern continent, while in the polar regions the seabed and the tundra were releasing gases that would increase the global temperature even further. In space, a satellite that was still in use had collided with the remnants of a deactivated satellite, or perhaps it had been blown to pieces in a military test, greatly increasing the amount of space debris in orbit and making space launches even more risky.

16

FIVE-FORTY. IT WAS TIME TO GO. HE PUT ON HIS
jacket, shouldered the backpack, and approached the counter.
The cook held out a small payment terminal to him.

"Thank you," he said when the payment had gone through.

"My pleasure," the cook said. "Receipt?"

He shook his head. "No need."

"Stay warm," the cook said, "it's a cold night."

"Thanks," he said, "I will."

The air was cold, yet it lacked real teeth and felt more like late
September than mid-November, except for the early twilight.
The darkness of winter was intruding upon an autumn that
seemed to have no plans of leaving.

The wind pushed him one more street away from the pier,
and further along the sea, to a brown-painted door wedged
between the unlit displays of a surf shop (surfboards, shorts,
and shirts with flower prints in primary colors) and a pharmacy
(sun tan lotions, hair care products with sun protection factor,
sunglasses, and band-aids). He expected the door to be locked,
but it slid open without a sound and led up a narrow, worn flight
of stairs to a corridor. There, about ten people in rain coats and

fleece jackets were standing in the warmth and humidity caused by wet clothes and poor ventilation. None of the people were familiar to him, so he squeezed past them without worrying about being recognized. Further down the hallway one vending machine offered coffee, espresso, latte, and chocolate milk, while another had bottles of mineral water, soda, chocolate bars, small bags of chips, and mixtures of nuts. Past the snack dispensers were several open doors and another small crowd clearly waiting for the lectures to start. He pretended to study the food and drinks in the vending machines, while he glanced at the small crowd. Some were catching up with each other and exchanging personal news as they dispersed into the meeting rooms, others were standing alone in the corridor, reading the notice boards or newspapers they had brought, or their phones. More people arrived from the stairs and greeted the others, a few with breath that smelled of liquor and food.

When most of the crowd had vanished into the first room and he heard a voice urging people to find seats, he chose a drink from the vending machine, a lemon-flavored soda he hadn't had in years. After the salty dinner something sweet would be nice. The bottle fell from its perch behind the plastic and down into the bottom with a thud. He unscrewed the lid slowly to allow the excess carbon dioxide to escape and avoid drawing attention to himself during the talk, and took a sip of the overly sweet liquid. Then he entered the small lecture hall and sat down in the back. From the low dais at the head of the room Narayan was introducing the speaker of the evening.

When Kaye entered from a doorway behind Narayan and took the microphone from the graduate student, he slid further down his seat to hide behind the rest of the audience. He searched Kaye's face and hands for scars from the owl, but from where he sat he couldn't see any. Even though Kaye turned out to be an experienced lecturer with a clear voice and diction, speaking not too slowly and not too quickly, he was too distracted to catch all of it. Kaye talked about commercial fish species no longer breeding enough to be harvested, how fish farming required fish as feed itself and was no substitute for wild varieties, how scientists had known about the overfishing for decades and tried to limit them, but had been ignored and silenced by the authorities and fishing companies, how few species were still present along the coast, and how fishing towns and communities all over the continent and on the other landmasses were vanishing due to lack of work and job opportunities. How the government had green-lighted drilling for oil and gas by global companies near the spawning grounds of protected and commercial fish species, how the protests from the local communities and environmental organizations had had miniscule effect on these decisions. How it was time to do something about the mess, not just sit on their asses and cry over it.

At the end of the lecture the audience was applauding and yelling; he wasn't certain what about, but he didn't want to be the only person in the room not clapping and smiling, so he cheered too.

17

THE MEETING ENDED WITH AN ANNOUNCEMENT
about the next lecture, at the same hour and weekday some
weeks into the future. He wasn't certain if he wished to travel
several hours for another glimpse of Kaye, but at least now
he knew the assistant professor was seemingly in good health.
When the audience stood and started trickling toward the door,
he pulled on his moist jacket and backpack and moved quickly
to exit before the main cluster of people. He reached the hallway without anyone calling after him, hurried down the stairs
and out into the night.

With the spectacle of the forested foothills and steep gorges
hidden inside the night, the journey back to the mountains was
long and tedious. Now the glass surfaces only reflected what
went on inside the compartment, like the exclusively internal
images of the sleeping mind.

Finding himself alone in the compartment he called Michael,
who answered almost immediately.

"How are things in the mountains?" Michael said.

"They're good," he smiled. "Quiet, but rainy. How are things
at home?"

"Fine, fine," Michael said. "Windy. Had a big storm earlier this week, with thunder and lightning. Lots of trees fell down, power lines and roads blocked, roofs ruined. The wind and the tide took half the beach in the bay, they had to cover the sand with branches from old pines to prevent more from washing away. It was a proper fall storm, only not much colder than in the summer. Did you see it on the news?"

"I missed that," he said, feeling a pang of guilt. "How are your parents? No one injured, I hope."

"No, no worries, everyone's all right, just more difficult to move around in the city than usual. But the streets are being cleaned up quickly. Wait, is that a train I'm hearing in the background? Are you on your way home?"

At the joy in Michael's voice, his heart jumped and the regret for not having caught a train that continued further down the coast and back to the city seared him. "Sorry," he said and smiled into the phone. "I'm returning to the cabin. Just seen a doctor on the coast."

"A doctor?" Michael said. "Are you sick?"

"No, I'm fine. I was just getting a pilot license for the astronaut test."

"Astronaut test?" Michael laughed. "Are you going to the moon?"

"You know, for the astronaut training program. It's been in the news lots of times."

"Oh, that," Michael said. "Did you apply for it? How did it go?"

"I passed the first round," he said, and realized that Michael was the first person he had told this to. "They want to do a second series of tests. That's what the pilot license is for."

"Congratulations!" Michael said. "That's fantastic! Do you know how many rounds of tests there will be?"

"No," he said. "But the next time I think they'll wish to meet us in person. And there will probably be more medical tests, if my impression from the articles about the selection process is correct."

"Don't you dare come home for testing without stopping by," Michael said.

He smiled. "I promise."

"You are coming home for Christmas, aren't you?" Michael said.

"Yes, of course," he said, although it was the first time he had thought of Christmas since he arrived in the mountains. "We'll celebrate together, as always. How's Beanie, by the way? Is the building still standing? Not a smoking hole where the apartment used to be, or the pool leaking out the window?"

"No," Michael laughed. "Everything's still there, don't worry. Beanie loves the cats and they adore her. And she keeps the apartment surprisingly tidy, considering she lives there."

He laughed.

"I suspect she thinks you might suddenly come home for a surprise visit and doesn't want to be caught."

He laughed again. "Sometimes fear is the best taskmaster," he said.

Michael chuckled, then paused. "We miss you," Michael said. "Your brother says your father sounds ready to disown you if you don't come home soon."

"I don't understand the fuss," he said. "Father left his country when he was much younger than I am now. I'm still on the same continent as you, just a few hours away by train."

"Yes..." Michael said. "He's just concerned. I am too, I mean, all of us are. My parents, and Beanie too."

"I'm fine," he said. "I'm not going crazy, I haven't sold all my belongings. The neighbors just started a farming project sponsored by the ministry for agriculture. They might have a crop this spring already. I want to see how it develops."

"They're farming in the mountains?" Michael said.

"Yes, it's that warm now," he said. "Look, all of this is just temporary. Don't worry."

"I know," Michael said. "I know."

He needed a moment to compose himself before making the next call. That's what he disliked the most about phone conversations. They tended to derail, and without the direct interaction of facial expressions and body language, it was difficult to get back on track once that happened. He sighed, then tapped the number of his younger brother.

In the beam from his headlamp the path from the train platform to the cabin shone like exposed bone and the scent from the heather and bilberry was fragrant and strong. The wind was low and humid and there were no moon and no stars in the sky. He wondered what it felt like to shoot through that darkness for months, without being able to go outside, or take a breath of fresh air, or be with friends and family, of not seeing the places he loved or doing the things he usually did. But then the images of another place blossomed up in his mind. A mountain, the remnants of an enormous volcano, so huge its summit curved beyond the horizon, forever out of sight, halfway to the stars. A canyon so large it could hold three of the deepest gorges on Earth inside itself and still have room for more. Endless plains traced with the marks of long-forgotten rivers and deltas, superimposed by craters and calderas. An anaerobic, freezing wind blowing red. Going there, seeing those sights, landscapes that no human being had ever witnessed before, would be more than worth the danger, boredom, and loneliness of the journey.

In the shrub around him insects hummed and from overhead came the clicks and ticks of hunting bats. He remembered Kaye telling him that a bat, when petted, would purr loudly, like a cat.

18

THE TRUCKS AND TRACTORS AND CARS AND PEO-
ple arrived while the sky was still orange and the dawn clouds
heavy along the horizon. He sat up on the mattress, pulled out
of sleep by the noise and light. The convection from the tripartite window chilled him and he was sweaty and cold at the same
time, as if he'd spent the night outdoors. He yawned and rubbed
his face. He smelled of sleep and unkempt hair. If Michael had
been there, he would have made drowsy waking-up noises, muttered to him in a morning-hoarse voice.

The neighbors heaved large sacks from the trucks to the
ground, gathered around the bags, and began filling the seed
drills attached to three tractors. With the seeds loaded, the tractors started moving. One of them drove southwest, another
chugged north, and the last continued west for a short distance
before they changed gears and spat thick smoke from the chimneys. The vehicles entered the newly fertilized soil, sank a little
into it, before they continued slowly along the plowed furrows.

From the cabin he couldn't spot any trails of pale grains on
the ground; the seed drills probably placed and covered the
seeds as they advanced. The nearest tractor continued down the
field. A flock of seagulls, far from the coast, bobbed up and

down in the air, and sparrows, blackbirds, starlings, even a few ravens and lapwings, alit when the tractor had passed, trying to catch the seeds that had not been covered and the worms and bugs that had been churned up from the soil.

Someone banged on the door. He pulled the sleeping bag around him.

"Come in!" he said and turned toward the kitchen.

Eloise stood in the doorway, knee-high rubber boots soiled to the rim, the front of her green oilskin jacket spattered with mud, her cheeks red and her eyes shining like the sun in spring.

"We're starting," she beamed. "Finally we're off!"

"Want some tea?" he said.

She shook her head, too busy to stop. "Imagine, in just a few months all this will be covered by grain, ready to be harvested, to fill our stores, and to be packaged for export. And then, after the first harvest, we will be able to sow again almost immediately and have a second crop over the summer. This really is the future!"

He took the cup of water he always kept next to the mattress at night and toasted her. "To the future!" he said.

She looked at him and his naked chest, grew a little flustered, and folded her arms. "Not up yet?" she said.

"Not yet," he said, grinning.

She leveled her eyes at him, making no signs of leaving.

He gazed up at her. "The sowing is very noisy," he said. "How long will you be at it?"

She scoffed, turned, and slammed the door behind her.

Later in the day he received an email that the manual treadmill he ordered had arrived at the post office. He got up, washed, shaved, dressed, and ate, and emptied the large backpack. Then he walked for an hour and a half to the post office in the center of town, tied the cardboard box with the treadmill to his backpack with lengths of twine he pulled off a cone at the packing desk and cut with a flourish of the scissors that hung there.

He also purchased freeze-dried camping food: beef stew, lamb stew, vegetable stew, cod terrine, pasta in tomato sauce, ground beef in chili sauce, chicken in curry, tomato soup, pea soup, and oatmeal, and met no one he knew.

When he arrived at the cabin it had already grown dark, but the distant, shivering beams and the low, steady noise from at least two engines indicated that the neighbors were still at work. Would they carry on all night as they had done during plowing? Above the cabin's deck the sky was a black dome, pierced with stars.

Inside, he put the backpack down and untied the rectangular box fastened to it. He opened the container with the old, but still-sharp boxcutter from the kitchen drawer, and assembled the small steel construction with the simple tools that were included in the package. He had chosen a manual treadmill for easier transport, assembly, and storage. At day he could move the treadmill out on the deck and run even if it turned too muddy to jog along the fields, or if snow and ice arrived. Should he have another white-out, a manual treadmill would be safer than a motorized one.

He placed the mill by the panorama window so he could run and imagine being outside. Then he put on his trainers to test the acquisition. The oblong rubber surface had a pleasant give and moved comfortably along with his steps. He ran for almost an hour while he watched the tractors progress slowly from north to south and then back again along the plowed furrows, casting about headlights that were quickly consumed by the night. After the run he went to sleep on the mattress and dreamed that seagulls, sparrows, and blackbirds landed on him while stalks of ripe wheat grew forth from his flesh.

With the three seed drills and tractors the sowing took only a few days. Then the fields were still dark, but full of hidden, secret life, which would germinate over the winter and become sustenance, income, and a bulwark against starvation. What countless people in the world must be desiring. Seed banks and grain stores had been mentioned more and more frequently in the news. The word "stockpiling" hadn't come up yet, but he assumed that by now most countries were saving what they could, as well as recalculating their annual yields given the new numbers for yearly average precipitation and temperature. Many nations had started rationing water to ensure that the industry had what it needed. On the internet were rumors that some countries were pumping water that had already been used once by industrial facilities into the public water network, still full of heavy metals and other toxic compounds.

It was at least clear that the food prices had increased alarmingly and that an international race to purchase arable land and sources for water had been going on for quite some time. He assumed that corporations and individuals who could afford it would not only stockpile, but create gated enclaves, like revelers in the stories about the plague, to ensure access to the most vital resources. He also wondered whether his own move from the city to the cabin, and the neighbors' tilling and seeding, could also be regarded as such. But he thought not. It was safeguarding the future, taking active measures. Neither he nor the farmers were keeping anyone out or preventing them from leaving.

At first he enjoyed the idea of the seeds growing in the dark soil all around the cabin and turning the ancient nutrients of the earth and air into food. He dreamed of golden fields and the wind whispering in the grain, but when he realized that the first green stalks might soon peek like stubble through the substrate, he thought he hadn't searched far enough to secure a home in the wilderness. Nevertheless, with the sowing done, the cabin was just as isolated and the nights and days as silent as before. No road had been built, nor had any of the neighbors erected new buildings or created any constructions that imposed on his land. Worse yet, he had willingly accepted the tilling and sowing and signed the farmers' project. As when the plans had first been presented to him, he couldn't see any drawbacks, only advantages. The project would bring food, security, and possibly a steady income. But he disliked looking at the now-cultivated land so much that he turned the sofa, the mattress, and the treadmill away from the panorama view and toward the deck and the forest and the sky that was visible through the window in the kitchen and front door.

To further distract himself from the new and unsympathetic landscape, and although he usually feigned disinterest in the culture of his father's country, he ordered pale sand for the hearth especially selected and sieved by traditional craftsmen near the city of his grandparents. The sand originated from a beach where a historical battle had taken place and was flown to his country of residence. When the bag of ridiculously expensive sand arrived, he immediately walked over to Eloise and Mark's to borrow a shovel, and emptied the hearth of the old and dark sand. Then he hiked through the heather to the post office, carried the new sand home, and poured it slowly into the square pit in the floor.

Like a vampire finally in possession of soil from his ancestral lands to rest in, he spread the sand out in the hearth with his palms. When that was done he spent half the night picking up the pale and fine grains, and letting them fall through his hands, again and again.

19

THE WEEKS PASSED QUICKLY INTO THE DARKEST
days of winter. The temperature sank, but only to that of a mid-
autumn. He reserved a train ticket home for Christmas, with an
open return back to the mountains. Kaye's next lecture was only
a few days away. Now that he knew Kaye was alive, he hadn't
planned on attending the meeting, but as the date approached,
he realized that he had no reason not to go and knew that if he
didn't he would regret it. The last time he had managed to avoid
being spotted by Kaye or anyone else who might have recognized him. If he was careful about how and when he arrived
and left, there was no reason in the world he shouldn't remain
unseen.

He checked the schedule online and memorized the times
when the trains went back to the mountains, and ordered a
ticket. When that was done he felt elated, but also guilty, since
Michael would no doubt be hurt if he knew. He spent the rest
of the evening buying Christmas gifts online for Michael (photography and cook books, jazz and classical music, a return trip
from the city to the cabin by train), Beanie (high-end earphones,
five rolls of hard-to-find analog film, a spacious memory card
for her digital camera), Katsuhiro (a computer role-playing

game, science-fiction films, hair and skin care products), and his parents (matching bathrobes, a stone garden lantern from his father's country). He ordered everything gift-wrapped, attached with notes, and mailed to the post office nearest to the honeycomb towers so he wouldn't have to carry them in his backpack home.

Since he had no doctor's appointment this time, he caught a late train to the coast. When he arrived it was almost dark, a heavy, mist-filled dusk shrouding the town and the sea. Along the pier the ocean was a charcoal plain under a sky the same color, but quiet and still, not perturbed like on his last visit. Not even the cries of seagulls broke the hush. It reminded him of the descriptions of the land of the dead in classical literature; an ashen, cold, and silent world where the dead wandered restlessly, yearning for their former lives, under a sky where neither the sun nor the stars ever rose. Those descriptions had seemed more peaceful and less terrible than the images of the afterlife which the continent's dominant religion offered: burning in lakes of fire while being tortured by malevolent supernatural beings. But now he felt less certain. Perhaps eternal agony was preferable to eternal longing.

Darkness fell quickly. The resort town seemed almost abandoned, and more shops were closed or boarded up than last time. As he crossed the city center and entered the streets that led inland, he saw only a handful of moving cars. Not until he reached the brown-painted door between the surf store and the pharmacy where a handful of people stood smoking and chatting did he see anyone else. He stopped a few meters upwind from the group and checked his mail and messages on the phone. When the smokers dropped their cigarettes and filed inside, holding the door open for one another, he followed them into the threadbare corridor and up the stairs. Once again he had timed his arrival well, and while the crowd was about to sit down and hang their jackets on the backs of their chairs, he slid into a seat behind them. Right in front of him was a tall man in a red jacket and a woman with a hairy knit beret. If he leaned back in the chair, he'd be almost impossible to see from the front.

This time the introductory speaker wasn't Narayan, but a woman with blond hair he recognized as one of Kaye's senior PhD students. Were these lectures some form of graduate teaching? Or had Kaye moved his entire group to the coast to conduct marine research? But the graduate student presented no local projects or experiments of her own, only the reports and numbers of other scientists, research institutions, and international organizations, on climate change and global warming. How much the temperature was increasing, the speed at which it was happening, how fast the polar regions were melting, how quickly the sea was rising, how much the heightened levels of carbon dioxide in the atmosphere increased the acidity in the oceans and the thawing of the tundra, how the new temperatures led to droughts, forest fires, crop failures. How the elevated ocean levels made low-lying cities and countries prone to flooding, storms, loss of drinking water, and arable land, how food production was dramatically decreasing all over the world, and how, in just a few years only the truly rich would be able to afford to eat food that was clean and healthy, while starvation, malnutrition, and lack of water would become the norm for most of the planet's billions, even on the western and northern continent. The student then showed what the rainier summers and the milder winters in the north and the hotter summers and the drier winters in the south would mean for the countries on the continent. It was no longer a question of if or when, the changes were not about to happen, they had long since started, and already the effects of human-made climate change were being felt harshly all over the planet.

The information made his stomach turn and his heart beat heavily. He remembered warnings in the past of how bad the future would become if the emissions of greenhouse gases were not ceased or the use of fossil fuels not exchanged for renewable energy sources. That had not happened, they had been allowed to continue more or less like before, and so the troubling, uncertain future had become the volatile, menacing present.

Finally, Kaye himself appeared on the dais and took the microphone. More slides and graphs, what the climate and environmental changes would mean for the country, this particular stretch of coast, and the local community. And lastly, what the community could do, which political representatives to write to, what companies to protest against, which rallies to join, and petitions to sign, what a grassroots movement could do, and was allowed to do.

Kaye made it sound like it did matter, that it would actually help. He felt like joining those petitions, writing those politicians, returning to these meetings. When the lecture was over, he was so caught up in the buzz and the chatter of the crowd that when he finally rose to leave, the aisle was thronged with people and the doorway blocked. He cursed inside for having lost his presence of mind and not left earlier. He quickly put on his jacket and folded the collar up. It was an average mountain jacket from a very common brand. He had seen at least one other like it in the crowd, so theoretically he should not be noticed. But the queue moved slower than passengers exiting a plane, the audience busy hailing each other and chatting amicably, discussing the lecture and recent local events. He had forgotten to take the slow trickle of familiarity into account.

He was nearly jumping with impatience when someone called his name from behind and moved toward him with quick steps. There was no point in trying to pretend that he hadn't heard it, and the crowd was moving so slowly there was no chance to slip out the door and get away. Forcing himself to relax, telling himself he already had the back story he needed, he turned.

"What a pleasure to see you here," Kaye said, beaming. Faint vertical scars were visible just beneath his hairline.

"Kaye," he said, "that was one hell of a presentation."

Kaye laughed and patted his shoulder. "Thank you, my friend," he said. "Environmental protection has always been a passion of mine. These days it's no longer about conservation, but of survival."

He suddenly remembered one of the awards and certifications that had been on display in Kaye's house. "Now I understand why the faculty named you best lecturer of the year," he said, smiling. But instead of the immediate and distracting shine the flattery was meant to produce, there was a brief sting, a visible guardedness in Kaye's eyes.

"Thank you," Kaye said and returned the smile, a little too late to look unforced. "But what are you doing in this part of the world? Don't tell me you're here on vacation, this time of year?"

He shook his head. "No, I'm here for a doctor's appointment. I live up at the moor now."

"You've given up the city?" Kaye chuckled. "I always figured you for an urbanite."

He smiled again. "I got mixed up with an agricultural project and some crazy farmers."

"So you're a farmer now?" Kaye said and laughed.

"It seems so," he lied.

"Now I'm curious, what's this project about?"

"Winter wheat," he said.

"Winter wheat? In the mountains?"

He nodded.

"You know, they used to get most of their money from logging."

"Seems they want to expand their business," he said. "It's become mild enough to grow other crops."

Kaye's smile faded. "See how far it's been allowed to develop? And the worst thing isn't that it's our fault, our capitalism, our consumption, and our unwillingness to stop it that's made it so. The worst thing is that we saw it coming decades ago and we barely did anything, because of our self-interest and refusal to change. We had every chance, all the possibility in the world to stop it in time, and we didn't take it. Future generations are going to view us as the ancestors who permanently ruined the environment."

He looked down and nodded. Kaye's thoughts were familiar. "So what can we do about it?" he said. People flowed past them and out, trailing behind them the sour smell of moist clothes and perspiration. From the open door a chilling draft blew in from the night.

"There's plenty we can do," Kaye said. "The world's just waiting for us to do it. Is your email address still the same?"

"Yes, it is," he said. If Kaye had had his address all this time, why hadn't he mailed?

"Good," Kaye said, backing up toward the dais. "I have to run now, finish things up here. Thanks for coming to the meeting. I'll send you an email shortly, it's easier to explain in private."

"Thanks," he said. "Do you live here, by the way?"

"No," Kaye said, turning away from him. "Talk with you soon."

He let the crowd carry him out the door and down the stairs. Outside, it was dark and quiet and the familiar drizzle had started again. The rest of the audience vanished into the night one by one and two by two, and soon there was just him and the pier and the waves that surged in from far out at sea.

20

THE NEXT DAY, HAVING MET KAYE SEEMED LIKE A dream. He could barely remember what Kaye had said and what he had said and why. Yet he knew he hadn't said what he'd imagined saying if Kaye recognized him, and he hadn't said what he most wanted to. There had been too many people around for that. He ought to have asked Kaye to talk in private, but since Kaye had been busy, his students and co-speakers waiting for him, it had seemed that Kaye would say no, so he hadn't done that. Next time, he thought. Next time they would chat more and he would say what he needed to.

And Kaye was not living on the coast? Where was he staying? Still in the city? Then why was he holding lectures out of town? The assistant professor could easily have gotten twice the audience at the university, particularly if he was still popular among the students.

He slept until the afternoon sun woke him by brightening the panorama window and gleaming above the mountains in the west. He got up, turned on the laptop, and checked his mail. No new messages.

He changed into training clothes and shoes, and ran along

the fields, whose edges were more clearly defined and drier than before. The air was chilly. With the heather and bilberry shrub gone, their gamey fragrance had been replaced by something less wild and more familiar: soil and dirt. In the distance a flock of sparrows lifted from the ground, but he hadn't seen as large a gathering as that which had warmed him earlier in the fall. The sunlight was sharp but pale, and he turned his face toward it to soak up what little warmth it held.

When he returned to the cabin the sun had already sunk to darkness. He kicked off his muddy trainers, left them on the deck to dry, and went inside to wake the laptop from its sleeping mode. No new mail. He returned outside, attached the rubber hose to the tap, undressed, and showered in the cold water on the veranda. Then he dried, threw the moist t-shirt, sweatpants, and socks up on the banister, and hurried back to the warmth inside.

There he pulled on soft indoor clothes: a pair of faded light blue jeans, a white t-shirt, and a gray cardigan he had borrowed from his father. He checked the mail again before he filled the old pot with water and made oat porridge with blueberry jam. After he had eaten he found a couple of IQ tests online, and completed them as fast as he could. He assumed similar tests would be part of the astronaut selection process. When he needed a break, he put on the headlamp, went outside to the pile of logs he had stacked against the southern wall, and retrieved a few. The pile was down to twenty or thirty pieces of pale birch trunk speckled with black. He doubted the neighbors would be happy if he cut down the few birches that were left between the fields, so he would have to hike to the town center for more fire-wood. Besides, it would be nice to have a swim in the municipal pool, the ocean was far away and he missed it. The town pool would make a decent substitute, although it wouldn't be as pri-vate as the one at home.

He returned inside, placed the logs in the hearth, and lit them with the lighter from the top drawer in the kitchen. As his breath and body settled, he stared into the flames for a long while. Then he checked his mail once more, before he undressed, and went to bed in the sleeping bag on the mattress. Right before he fell away the white light flared up inside him, engulfing him. Then there was nothing he lacked, nothing he had to do. It was a break from the world and its concerns. It happened every night, a quiet reset back to himself. Only when the morning arrived would he once again grow a body and mind and become human again.

21

IN HIS DREAMS THE OCEAN WAS ILLUMINED BY ITS
own clarity, as the enlightened mind is said to be. The brightness
seared him. It was so cold the sea surface was sluggish with ice.
His right hand ached. He thought of the screws and plates that
had been drilled into his fingers and joints when he broke them
last summer and how the metal now must be contracting in the
polar conditions.

The ship that carried his parents and brother and him was
white and colonial-looking, of the type he had seen in old movies about murders on the broad rivers of the southern continent. His family members pushed open the round-eyed door
of the cabin to a wall of icy, dazzling air. All around them the
ocean bristled with the frost-bearded masts and chimneys of the
countless vessels it had caught.

"Your father and I have been invited to dine with the cap-
tain," his mother said. She was dressed in a red silk gown and
looked like she had in her mid-thirties, decades ago.

"Which one of them?" his brother said. Katsuhiro was of his
current age and wearing the navy-blue oilskin jacket that hung in
the hallway at home in the honeycomb towers.

"No, no, your mother and I need to have something to

ourselves," his father said, also much younger than in waking life, dressed in his best morning coat, with his black hair slicked back as he had in pictures from his twenties. They watched their parents vanish up the canvas-flanked stairs to the top deck.

"I'll follow them, find out where they're going," Katsuhiro said.

"No, don't," he said. "They'll be back soon. We can do something else in the mean time."

His brother pouted in reply, then continued to the deck below.

There was a rush in the air, a warmth and a glow, as if the sun had managed to burn through the clouds. On the mattress, far, far away, he felt a pull, an attraction, like that which works between two magnets, but was unable to change or cease the dream. With a keening wail a plane shot past him and into the still, bright water. The airliner crashed down with almost no splash, and sank with the sound of the passengers' desperate screams behind the windows barely audible and very far away. The fear in the crowd's faces as they fought to break out of the sinking plane, and the knowledge that they would not, was louder and more piercing than their cries for help. As the plane turned like a sleepy whale in the water and sank into the luminous depths, the sea gave only a single ripple as acknowledgment of the disaster before it grew still.

Out on the white plain of frozen, half-sunken wrecks that was the graveyard ocean, one or two steel bodies gently moved and creaked as if in sympathy with, or in domino-effect from, the new arrival. The frost and ice on the jutting bows and piercing masts were snot-yellow, as was the color of their sun-bleached paint. He even spotted the rotund outline and mesh body of an airship out there, yet even in the dream he knew that few airships had ever made it to the sky, much less the polar regions.

As he watched the overcast pale heavens, another plane came down, roared past just above his head, spewing a desperate heat and the stench of gasoline on fire like the draft from a barbecue grill in the summer. He ducked and turned to follow the descent. The fuselage broke up in a shower of smaller pieces before it hit the water, then sank as discreetly and as quietly as the plane that had preceded it. This time he was too far away to hear the screams and cries of the passengers, and was grateful for that.

Almost immediately one of the many cruise ships that roamed the water's ice-swollen surface, weaving carefully in and out between the wrecks, steered toward the remnants of the fallen. The side of the ship that faced the now-burning victim fuselage was filled with passengers who pointed and yelled to announce the disaster to their fellow travelers. But no life boats were lowered, no life jackets hurled into the still water, no mayday sent out, because they were all there voluntarily, enjoying the sight of the jetsam going down and thanking the multitude of gods that it wasn't them. As the frozen wrecks out on the oceanic plain rearranged themselves once more to make room for the newcomer another cruiser approached the recent crash.

But beneath him, the ship he was on was also slowly going down. It was already up to the mid-deck railing in bright teal waves. He gazed into the liquid stillness and saw people in evening finery swim from the ship's windows and out into the searing water. He wondered if his brother and parents were among them, but refused to follow the escaping passengers with his eyes. Instead, he noticed that streams of bubbles were bursting forth from the windows on the lower decks because they had loosened in their frames from the chill and insistency of the ocean.

Now the upper deck had nearly drowned, as if the ship voluntarily let the sea into itself and was embracing it, instead of fighting to keep it out and remain on the surface. Cold wavelets nipped at his naked feet, and he hurried to climb a steel ladder on the wall of the bridge. Another sunken ship was close.

Sometime in the past it had settled peacefully on the bottom and now only peeked the apex of its bow, a corner of the roof, and the tallest of its masts above the ice. As he prepared to jump to the other wreck, he saw that other cruise ships were approaching the vessel he was about to leave. They were all ablaze in the flashlight from a thousand cameras, going off to no avail in the bright ocean-light, eager to watch the sinking of the others while already taking in water themselves.

He woke up feeling more tired than when he went to bed, and bleary-eyed from too much sleep. The first thing he did was turn on the laptop and check his mail. A jolt of tension shot through him. There was a message from Kaye:

> My dear friend,
>
> I'm so glad you made contact. I sense that you wished to talk more about my work and current situation. This makes me delighted as there are many opportunities with us, which I would be very happy to see you take up.
>
> I'd like to speak with you again in the new year. Please advise.

At first he was so elated that Kaye wanted to meet again that he didn't reflect on the letter. But as the initial joy receded, he read the mail again and again and found the tone and wording businesslike and stiff, not at all like the brief, informal messages they had exchanged in the city. He wasn't certain what Kaye wanted from him, but he was too happy not to reply with a date and time to meet.

22

HE DREADED GOING HOME FOR CHRISTMAS, TO the city, to his family, to the questions, but he had promised Michael and Katsuhiro that he would.

He phoned Beanie to let her know he was planning to return for a brief visit.

"You're coming home for Christmas?" Beanie said. "When? I'll stay with Andy over the holidays, he'll be pleased." Beanie laughed, sounding a little nervous. He imagined her glancing about in the apartment, assessing what had to be cleaned and how many days she had left till he was there.

"No need for that," he said. "I'll take the sofa. I'm just stopping by for a few days. I have to travel south right after New Year's."

"But it's your apartment, your bed," Beanie said.

"It's been your apartment for the last months," he said. "Just give me some clean sheets and the second duvet and I'll be fine."

"Are you sure?" Beanie sounded much less tense than before.

"Of course I'm sure," he said.

"All right. When will you get here?"

"I'll arrive the evening before the family dinner," he said. He didn't want to stay for long in the apartment when it was full of Beanie's belongings.

"Super!" Beanie said. "The cats and I will be waiting for you."

"How are they?" he said in order to move the conversation over to a less difficult subject.

"They have been absolute darlings," Beanie said. "Eating well, purring loudly, curling up to me in bed every night. I love them."

"I miss you all," he said and meant it.

"We've missed you too and I know the cats are looking forward to seeing you again," Beanie said. "We all are."

"I'm looking forward to seeing you as well," he said.

He wanted to call Michael too, but knowing that if he did, the second thing Michael would ask was how long he'd stay, stopped him. Beanie would disseminate the news anyway.

There wasn't much to pack. All his good clothes were in the apartment, the gifts he ordered had been sent to the post office in the train station by the honeycomb towers, and the winter and training clothes he had in the cabin would not be needed in the city. He took only the small backpack and it was half full at best, with clean underwear, his wool scarf, leather gloves, wallet, and phone. He walked to the train platform in the foredawn, following the path that snaked through the underbrush. The morning was cold and fog-filled, with a peculiar scent of expectation.

When the train arrived the cars were almost full and he had to push his way through three compartments before he found an empty seat behind two elderly couples that were playing cards. The seat was partially blocked by the seniors' many pieces of luggage, which there was no room for in the overfilled racks by the door. Even the shelf above the windows was full of bags and backpacks and clothing.

"Pardon me," he said, squeezing past the pensioners' suitcases. The far seat was hidden by thick coats and scarves hung on the hook by the window. He put his backpack on the floor and sat down in the aisle seat. As the train arrived at the stops along the coast, it became increasingly delayed and the compartment more and more crowded. In the warm and heavy air he fell asleep between the luggage and the passengers standing in the aisle. Outside, the day brightened slowly, but the light was gray and wan, and would remain only for a few hours. As opposed to earlier in the winter, now the trees in the valleys and the mountainsides were bare, with only the occasional green conifer.

When the train finally clacked into the central train station in his home city, in a web of glinting rails and overhead wires, it had grown dark and most of the passengers were asleep. He picked up his backpack, queued for the doors, and stepped out on the familiar concrete. The wall of noise from people and traffic, the orange glare from the sodium lamps, the scent of sweat, perfume, exhaust, and cigarette smoke, made his months in the mountains instantly vanish.

Another crowded, warm, and noise-filled train took him from the city central to the subterranean steel and glass corridors of the station by the apartment buildings. Bobbing with the crowd, not attempting to run ahead or lag behind, he moved with the throng out the tunnels, up through the park, and into the parking lots below the high-rises. The five six-sided structures rose nineteen floors above the asphalt, the illumination from their rows of windows glittering in the winter night.

He rang the doorbell and took out the keys, but Beanie opened the door before he could use them. She shrieked and threw her arms around him with such force that he stumbled backward and the red, white-trimmed velour hat she was wearing fell to the floor. Beanie smelled of licorice and cigarettes and the perfume from some jeans designer he couldn't recall the name of, but which he strongly associated with her, and hugged her hard.

He had hoped for a quiet evening before the big family dinner, but past the door, in the clearly newly cleaned and tidied apartment, stood Michael and Katsuhiro. They waited patiently until Beanie had pulled him inside and closed and locked the door, and when he could finally embrace Michael, it was like he had never been gone at all.

23

HE CAME BACK FROM SLEEP IN BLOCKS, FRAG-
ments of being. First he was an arm lying on top of the duvet
which the rest of his body slept beneath. Then, somehow, he
was the cobalt-colored glass lamp on the table at the end of
the sofa. After that he was cat paws stepping on his chest, and
finally, he was a face that woke up and took in the room.

The cat that approached him was the cream-colored one, the
smallest and gentlest of the two felines he shared the apartment
with. She sniffed his nose, and gave him slow, loving blinks with
her elongated, copper-colored eyes. He stroked her soft, warm
back and she purred loudly and kneaded the duvet with her
paws. The living room was silent and gray, and beyond his feet
that pressed against the armrest at the far end of the sofa shone
the window which filled the north wall. Beyond the glass was the
balcony, which didn't reach further out than the length of a small
table and two chairs, separated from the neighboring verandas
by narrow concrete walls. Above the tall glass railing the sky was
filled with clouds, looking like mist, thoughts, misconceptions.

When he lived in the apartment he used to enjoy lying on the
sofa, seeing nothing but the edge of the veranda ceiling and the
sky, and pretending he was in a parachute, a balloon, or a plane.

Now he might have the chance of actually living in the heavens, but in a vessel which would be hurtling toward another planet. The thought brought apprehension, a slight tightness in his chest, but also a rush of joy and excitement. What if he made it through the tests? What if he had the chance to go to Mars?

It would, of course, only happen after years, perhaps decades of learning, training, and simulating. First there would be the basic knowledge for astronauts: piloting, parachuting, experiencing high gravity in centrifuge and microgravity in parabolic flight, learning the general aspects and procedures of current spacecraft, launch systems, and orbital habitat. Then the more detailed and specialized knowledge of the function and structure of specific parts of the spacecraft and orbital habitat, training inside full-scale models and in underwater tanks, both at the astronaut facility of the continent's space organization and those on other continents. If he were selected for a mission, the training would be narrowed down to the specific needs for that flight: the scientific experiments, technological upgrades, or mechanical maintenance to be performed.

Mars itself would require at least half a year of traveling into the darkness, and a similar amount of time on the surface of the planet, which would be unknown, unfamiliar, despite the rovers and probes and orbiters that had already been there, to collect samples and carry out experiments, possibly to search for traces of liquid water and microbial life. Then another half year going back through the vastness of space, the orbit and trajectory arcing just right at the right time, what only species of a certain technological prowess, curiosity, and risk-taking could do. Would he ever come back? Would he even want to?

He shifted beneath the duvet, the cat lying flat on his chest with her paws curled up beneath her. She lifted her head and glanced at him, then squeezed her eyes together and blinked. She made it harder to breathe, but he had missed the warm presence of the feline and her thrumming, peaceful purring too much to move her. There was a loud meow and the other cat, who was larger and darker and more insistent, jumped up on the sofa. She strode across his belly and curled up on the duvet. The cream-colored cat moved to snuggle against the gray cat and create a chorus of purrs with her. He closed his eyes and a bolt of lightning rose up from his body to pierce him without pain. He let it burn and move as it wished, and fell into sleep to the sound of the cats.

When he woke again the apartment was still semi-dark and the clouds had dispersed to mist. Beneath the closed bathroom door a glow was visible and he could hear the shower going. Beanie was singing, a song he didn't recognize or catch the words to. The unfamiliar fragrance of her shower gel dispersed by the steam mixed with the scent of basil, rosemary, thyme, and parsley from the potted herbs that now crowded the kitchen counter, making the apartment feel like it truly belonged to someone else. He pulled the duvet with the cats still curled up together gently aside, rose, and knocked on the bathroom door.

"I'm done soon!" Beanie yelled.

"Take your time," he said. "I'll shower at the pool. But may I come inside for a towel?"

"Of course!" Beanie said. "And don't mind my singing."

He laughed and opened the brown door with a hand over his eyes, ducked into the steam and scent, and pulled a bath towel from the narrow shelves by the sink. The small iridescent tiles on the floor and walls were damp with moisture.

He brought only the towel, a bottle of liquid soap from his backpack, and a pair of sandals from the hallway in the apartment to the swimming pool. When he locked himself into the changing room he saw the clothes and shoes of another visitor on the white wooden benches. Maybe a Christmas guest or someone who used the day off to enjoy the pool. The four shower stalls were empty, their white oblong tiles shining in the light from the LED lamps in the ceiling. The window had no curtains or covering; that didn't seem necessary nineteen stories up and at an oblique angle to the next tower in the row.

He undressed and showered quickly, then hurried into the next room. The glass ceiling and walls gave him the same feeling of being in the sky as the view from his living room did. In the distance sat the high-rises of the city center and below the tower were the park, the rail line, and the dark wetlands which surrounded it. At night the illumination from the city would turn the sky and the marsh golden, but now they both looked gray and dull.

There was no one else swimming, no sign of the other visitor. They might be just using the gym next door. The lights in the room were off, but the illumination from the sky outside was more than enough to see by. He dove into the pool and swam fifty meters under water, two laps, while watching the white tiles and tiny sand particles glide past on the bottom. Living away from the pool had reduced his breath-hold, but he swam slowly and calmly for as long as he could, then went up for air before he had to. Then he swam another fifty meters under water and five hundred meters at the surface, halving his usual routine since he didn't want to be late. Finally, he floated on the water that slowly smoothed from the cessation of his motions. Outside it had started to rain, large, slow drops that tapped on the glass and wept down the window. Low-lying clouds surrounded the tower on all sides, so dense he could no longer see the ground.

24

AFTER THE SWIM HE RINSED WELL TO GET RID OF the weak yet pervasive smell of chlorine from his hair and skin, and returned to the apartment. It was humid and filled with multiple fragrances from Beanie's shower gel, shampoo, body lotion, and perfume. The bathroom door was ajar and the hair dryer was on.

"I'm back!" he shouted at the bathroom door. "Can I sneak into the bedroom to get some clothes?"

"Go ahead!" Beanie yelled over the dryer. "Your things are all there. I haven't touched them."

He smiled and hurried into the bedroom. The bed was undone and covered in layers of skirts, dresses, blouses, trousers.

"Let me guess, you have nothing to wear today?" he asked.

"Shut up!" Beanie replied.

With the bedroom closet full of his clothes, Beanie had installed a rack for storage next to it. The steel tubing was full of hangers holding blouses, sweaters, pants, skirts, and jackets in various colors, and the ends of stockings, scarves, belts, and socks spilled out of the half open drawers below. He had to step over three stacks of books, magazines, and vinyl records to reach the closet, and push more aside to open the doors. His clothes were still there, in the clean and folded shapes he had left them.

His brother Katsuhiro and Michael phoned, having arrived at the parking lot to pick them up.

"Come up for a drink first?" he asked.

"No time," Michael replied. "We're already late. Use a cattle prod on my sister to hurry her up."

He laughed. "I'll be downstairs right away."

When he opened the door to Katsuhiro's car, Michael stepped out and hugged him.

"It's so good to see you," Michael said, breathing on his neck.

He hugged Michael back and kissed him. Michael smelled of aftershave and newly steamed fabric and his face was very warm. In his skinny suit and narrow tie Michael looked great.

"We need to get Beanie," Michael said, "or we'll be standing here for half an hour more."

Michael took his arm and pulled him toward the entrance. The glass doors admitted them soundlessly. Inside, the foyer was brightly lit and empty, the air still and cold. Michael dragged him into one of the elevators, pushed the button, and kissed him hard. When they reached the floor they were both breathing quickly.

"Let's leave early tonight," he whispered. Michael nodded, eyes dilated and dark in the faint illumination in the hallway, and took his hand.

Michael opened the door and yelled, "Beanie! Five minutes, or we're coming in to fetch you!"

"Seven!" Beanie shouted from the bedroom.

"So how were the mountains?" Michael said with a neutral facial expression.

"A bit strange," he replied. "The neighbors have started growing wheat, it's gotten warm up there too."

"How do you stand it?" Michael said.

"The neighbors?" he said. "They're all right."

"No, being alone in that cabin, away from everywhere else, anyone else."

He laughed. "It's fine. The cabin's got everything a person needs, and it's quiet, peaceful."

"It's quiet and peaceful here as well," Michael said, looking at the apartment. "And the view is phenomenal."

"There's no traffic in the mountains," he said. "I can hear the wind at night and smell the heather in the morning."

"You look terrible," Michael said.

"I do?" he said. "I thought I looked fine."

"You've lost weight, and there are dark rings under your eyes."

"I'm training a lot," he said.

"How's that working out?" Michael asked.

"They called me in for a third test," he said, ignoring Michael's sarcasm. "Down south. Seems they wish to meet us in person, and do some medical exams."

"If you are being selected, how long will you be gone?"

"I don't know," he said. "It's a long training program, taking place with all the major space organizations, all over the world."

"You want to become an astronaut but you don't know how long it takes to go to Mars?"

"A year and a half," he said. "At best."

"One way or round trip?"

"Round trip."

Michael's eyes grew more and more dark. Then he blinked quickly and glanced down at his watch. "Five minutes, we're coming in, Beanie!" Michael strode over to the bedroom door and opened it.

Beanie shrieked and tried to keep them out. She was dressed in a twinkling sequin blouse and a short, wide skirt that reminded him of ballet dancers, only it was black. She was even in high-heeled shoes, but kept fiddling with a pair of large crystal earrings that reached almost to her shoulders.

"You're coming with us now," Michael said, picked her up, and put her over his shoulder. Working out or running on the nights his job as a financial risk analyst in the city allowed for, Michael had no problem lifting his petite sister.

"My earrings! I'm not finished yet!" Beanie yelled and flailed, but Michael continued into the hallway.

"Take her coat," Michael said, "we're late."

As soon as Katsuhiro saw them he started the car, having been their get-away driver many times before.

He got into the back seat and opened the other door from inside. Michael deposited Beanie, tucked her flaring skirt inside the vehicle, and closed the door, then took the passenger seat in the front.

"Everybody inside, including Beanie's skirt?" Katsuhiro said.

"Just about," Michael said and pulled on the seatbelt.

"You bastards!" Beanie yelled. "I lost my earrings! They were so expensive!"

"Don't forget that you and I have the same parents," Michael said.

"You're still a bastard," Beanie said.

Katsuhiro brought the car into a wide curve on the nearly empty parking lot and started down the road toward the motorway.

It was nearly dark. The honeycomb towers shrank behind them, but even from a distance he could see that more than half the balconies were unlit, several windows seeming to lack curtains. Katsuhiro had moved out early in the spring because of the high cost of living in the building. He wondered how many others had done the same.

They drove westward to one of the oldest residential areas in the city, where tall corkscrew hazel and hawthorn hedges hid long, low houses with flat roofs, expansive windows, and large wooden decks. Katsuhiro eased the car slowly into the driveway, then slipped it neatly around the corner behind the dense hedge which blocked even the view of the garage from the quiet street outside.

When he exited the car and started on the short path to the house, he saw that the low boxwood plant which stood in a wedge-shaped, glazed pot outside the front door had been cut into a tight sphere, garlanded with tiny string lights, and strewn with fake snow for an extra festive appearance. He nearly laughed when he saw it, and imagined Michael's father kneeling in front of the pot as if in worship, laboring to trim the bush into the perfect holiday ball. But it was an honest effort, as were the lit torches that flanked the rain-glistening shale paving toward the front door.

They were among the last to arrive, the hallway and the living room and kitchen full of Michael and Beanie's grandparents, aunts, uncles, and cousins, and their partners and children. Since his parents had no relatives in the city, they spent the holiday with Michael and Beanie's family. Fortunately, there were enough people for him to quietly fade into the background, and only have to muster small talk with a few people.

At the dinner table, beneath the sparkling chandelier and the Christmas garlands, relatives dressed in silk and sequins, velvet and fine wool, took turns clinking their cutlery against their glasses, standing up, and relating to the rest of the family what the past year had brought to themselves, their spouses, children, and pets. He refused to pay attention to the boring stories about who the family members had proposed to or married or given birth to, what they had bought or won or otherwise accomplished, and allowed his mind to relax while keeping his eyes open and his lips curved amicably upward. He was deep in his own thoughts when Katsuhiro tinkled a glass, rose, and started recounting their father's achievements and those of their mother and of Katsuhiro himself from the year that was almost through, things he hadn't heard before. But then Katsuhiro said, "And lastly, but not least, my beloved brother applied for the space organization's new astronaut training program and has already passed the two initial rounds. If this continues he may be the first of our family to go into space!"

Michael and Beanie's relatives oohed and aahed and toasted him and said, "We didn't know you had applied, how exciting, when's the launch?" He didn't even have to answer them, all he needed to do was to keep smiling through the surprise and irritation that had risen in him, and mumble something or other, and soon enough, another relative banged on their glass with their knife, and stood to recount their branch of the family's highlights of the year.

After dessert, but before the cognac, coffee, and cake, he snuck out to the hallway and pretended to be waiting for the bathroom while checking his phone for messages to get a break from the chatter and the hot air. His father appeared in the living room doorway and congratulated him on his success with the testing, and his mother beamed at him, hugged him, and said, "We are immeasurably proud of you and we love you!"

He wanted to invite Michael to the apartment to talk, but at the end of the evening Michael and Beanie stayed behind at their parents' house, and Katsuhiro drove him back to the towers alone.

"Did you really have to tell everyone about the astronaut program?" he said when they were almost there.

"Why not?" Katsuhiro said, pouting a little in the same way he did when they were small and he wasn't allowed to follow his older brother. "If I hadn't, you never would have told them."

"Of course not, that's my damned point!" he said.

"You are much too modest of your achievements," Katsuhiro said. "You have nothing to be ashamed of."

He turned and glared at the night-dark streets that rolled past them.

"Why does everything with you have to be so secret?" Katsuhiro asked. "If people disapprove of what you do, will that make you refrain from doing it?"

"No, only from telling you about it," he said and went back to watching the city.

25

THEY SLIPPED INSIDE THE SHADOW FROM THE
heat and humidity outside, where it seemed as if the August
warmth had caused the air to thicken and vibrate with the fre-
quency of the cicadas' song. The gloom enveloped them in a
fragrance of lotus incense and worn wood, with a musty undertone he couldn't quite place.

"Stand still," Katsuhiro whispered in the language of their
birthplace, not the tongue of the country they were visiting, that
of their father and his family. "Our eyes will adjust to the darkness in a few seconds."

"Don't worry," he growled, annoyed at being instructed by
his brother, who was two years younger and a full head shorter
than himself. "I won't trip over anything."

Katsuhiro nevertheless took hold of his sleeve.

His shirt, although thin, stuck to his back with perspiration,
and his heart beat slowly and heavily, as if his blood had thick-
ened from the heat. Carefully, so as not to make a sound, he
unscrewed the cap on the bottle of water he had bought in a
corner store on the way to the shrine. But as he tilted the nearly
empty plastic container back, it sloshed noisily.

"What the hell!" Katsuhiro hissed and tried to slap his hand. "Are you drinking inside a shrine?"

He knew Katsuhiro would do that, so he turned away and switched the bottle to his left instead. "At least I'm not swearing in one," he said, and downed the last of the water.

Katsuhiro hit his shoulder instead. In the glare from the open door, they could see a robe-draped silhouette lift its head and turn toward them, but the monk didn't say anything or approach them.

"Let's have a look, then," he whispered and sauntered further inside while pretending he didn't see the sweaty footprints his socks left on the wooden floor. Both he and Katsuhiro had removed their shoes and placed them on the rack outside before they entered the shrine, and they never wore shoes indoors, neither at home nor at their grandparents'. There was just enough light to spot the display which housed the relic and the sturdy pillars that flanked it in the back of the shrine. Even here, away from the sun, it was so hot and humid it was hard to breathe, and he deeply regretted that he had agreed to go to a country where the air grew warmer than the inside of his own body.

At the relic a crowd of candles flickered in the faint breeze from the door, their smoke rising and mixing with the fragrance from multiple bowls of incense. The reliquary itself was a box-like structure, approximately one meter in each dimension, fronted by a pane of uneven glass. In its scuffed and dim surface, the candle flames quivered and gleamed. He gazed at the small space for a while before realizing that it contained a human skeleton sitting cross-legged and draped in the silk robes and tall headpiece of a monk.

Before he could feel surprise that the shrine housed a mummy instead of a more common sacred object, and wonder why it had been sanctified, the scent of tea leaves and tree resin filled his nose and mouth, making him nauseous and dizzy. He staggered backward, cold sweat blooming on his forehead and back, and the urge to throw up, shrine or no shrine, to rush back to the hotel, and spend the rest of the day in the bathroom, overtook him. His pulse roared in his ears and he balled his hands into fists to regain some control of his body. On the other side of the glass, the skeleton's eye sockets were deep and lightless and the bone ridges above them were as black and smooth as the edge of a lacquered bowl.

He had started by eating only certain local nuts and seeds for a thousand days. Since he had been a vegetarian for most of his life, and the nuts and seeds were often used in the monks' dishes at the temple, the change was mild.

In the mornings he would participate in the daily tasks at the temple, as he had done since initiation: cleaning the floors, laundering robes, preparing the meals, sweeping the grounds. In the afternoons he ran for hours on the paths that wound through the forest, and in the evenings his meditations were extended. In the beginning it reminded him of his novice years, when the work had felt heavy, the food monotonous, the sitting raw, but then, as now, the structuring of the days, the slow rhythm of the seasons, and the yearly observances approaching and receding in turn, transformed the labor into something joyful and satisfying.

The minimized diet and the increased activity made him lighter, leaner, and not just in mass or weight, but in thoughts and concerns as well. They simplified everything further than taking the robes already had. He could easily see why the process was done and why it was given such reverence. It also built the endurance — and discipline necessary for the next part of his journey.

After a thousand days he was allowed to restrict his diet further, to only the bark and roots of pines that grew in the mountains above the temple complex. Every morning he ran to those heights to harvest the thick bark and bulbous roots with a small sickle and spade, in sun as in rain, never taking more than he would need for the coming day and be able to prepare on his own. On that thin, but fragrant diet, the soft parts of his body slowly shrank and vanished. Since his bones remained the size they had always been, they jutted the fabric of his robes to new and unexpected shapes, like the gorges that remain after a river has carved its way through.

When his flesh had finally become lean enough, he was permitted by the senior monks to go to the grove of droopy-leaved lacquer-sap trees to the north. He walked there with a broad knife and a deep bowl, cut a diagonal groove in the bark of a young tree, caught the drops of yellow-gray liquid that seeped forth in the bowl, and carried it back. In his room he heated water from the temple's sacred source in a bronze kettle patterned with long-stemmed poppies suspended from the claws of a small bronze dragon. He poured a little of the hot water into the resin he had collected, along with some tea leaves. The resulting infusion was bitter and thin, but he drank it while chanting scripture in his mind.

The effect from the sap tea did not delay, and voided his body in long, slow shudders that lasted through the night. When dawn finally arrived he was emptied and exhausted and drenched in his own sweat. The thought that he would have to return to the grove and do it all over again in just a few hours brought such despair that for the first time since he started the journey he considered leaving it, despite the shame that would entail.

With the second bowl he was already dehydrated when he started, and he could feel it damaging his insides a little more. When the sun finally paled the mountains to the east again, he was certain the other monks had heard every gag and groan he made during the night.

He thought his body would adjust to the water-removing tea the same way it had grown used to the reduction of sustenance during the two thousand previous days, but that did not happen. Instead his body seemed to become more and more sensitive to the sap, until even just the smell when he lifted the bowl to his mouth made him gag, and it was only through great labor, merciless detachment, and harsh discipline, that he managed to drain it. He usually started vomiting and perspiring long before the bowl was empty. He voided himself and drank more, retched and returned to the tea, until the bowl was empty. After that, the heaving went on for most of the night and into the morning, until it was time to push his legs beneath him and walk to the lacquer sap trees again. Once, while crossing the garden, he suddenly had to lean over the carefully raked leaves, but nothing came, not even bile, which saved him from a lifetime of shame for having soiled the temple grounds.

However, one morning when the snow was bearing down on the eaves and the chill swallowed every waft of heat from the brazier in his room, it came to him that the lacquer tree sap wasn't poison, but medicine. Not for the ills of the world, but for his own sickness of selfish desire and willful ignorance. After that he took the tea almost with pleasure.

His wrists and ankles thinned to twigs, his ribs and spine to branches. His skin became dry and thick, like parchment, and his lips paled and cracked. When he sat, it felt like the ends of his pelvic bone would pierce through his rump, and he was too weak to fulfill any of his tasks, even walking to the grove for more sap. Now that had become the chore of another monk. What little he could do, which was leaving his bedding to sit for a while and then lie down again, had to be done slowly and carefully, while looking beyond the constant ache in his bones, the listlessness in his limbs, the tenderness of his eyes. It caused every thought and emotion to stand out with cruel clarity, like a leafless tree under the desert sun, which did help the sitting.

Occasionally, the abbot handed him one of the tiny tangerines from the well-tended trees in the south garden, to stop his gums and skin from bleeding. He ate the golden fruits whole, peel and all, but where they had previously tasted sweet and fresh, now their scent and flavor was that of the sap tea and his own bile, and made him throw up and perspire almost as hard as they did. But he had to continue. Nearly no one who attempted the journey succeeded, and for those who did the rest hardly mattered.

The new year observances came and went and he barely noticed it. He scolded himself for his lack of attentiveness and presence of mind, but lost it again as soon as the voiding started with a mouthful of the next bowl of tea. No one suggested he cease the process; it would be the same as saying that they didn't think he'd manage, and being allowed to start on it was a sign of great trust and confidence, although on moonless nights when he slept with his head nearly in a bowl for voiding, he almost hoped someone would say something. Yet, in the spring he discovered a brightness, a glow inside himself, that was beautiful and terrible at the same time. He had no words for it and did not try to explain it, but remained inside it when he could, and simply watched it when he couldn't. He told no one of this.

When they finally moved him into his appointed space, built especially for his long limbs, he was more dead than alive. If it hadn't been for the stone behind him that supported his back and the wood around him that braced his knees, he would not have been able to sit up at all. No longer having to eat or drink was a relief since his insides refused everything now, even pure water from the temple's icy source. The silk ribbon they tied to his wrist extended to a small silver bell outside. He had to ring it once a day to signal he was still alive and that they shouldn't open his tomb yet to see if the transformation was complete. Since he couldn't see the sunlight through the stone and no longer managed to follow the passing of the days, he listened for the sounds of the morning chants instead, and rang the bell when they were done.

He didn't know how the end would come, but imagined it like falling asleep without noticing, which he had done all his life, or as something common, yet unstoppable, as the first snow in winter, or when the ice melts in spring. Now the brightness was there all the time and there was no need to leave it.

Katsuhiro said his name and he startled, nearly sending the plastic bottle that was still clenched in his hand clattering to the floor.

"Poor bastard," Katsuhiro said, nodding at the monk behind the glass. "Mummifying himself and then being buried alive."

"Why?" he said, his voice more high-pitched than he had intended. "He wanted to be happy. What more does human life have to offer?"

Katsuhiro stared at him. "That's crazy! Don't tell me you would have become a mummy too if you had lived back then?"

"Mind your own business," he said and started walking toward the door and the summer-sound of insects.

For weeks afterward Katsuhiro sent him photos of rich teenagers drinking champagne in private jets, shopping for designer goods with crowds of friends, or tanning by the pool on yachts while deep kissing other people. He never replied to those mails and immediately deleted them.

26

WITH THE NEXT ROUND OF TESTS FOR THE ASTRO-
naut selection program taking place right after New Year's, he
not only had a timely, but also an impressive-sounding excuse to
leave the city earlier than he otherwise would. Although Beanie
was staying over at her parents' house, probably in the girly-
looking bedroom where she grew up and which her parents still
kept, despite her having moved out years ago and having lived
in various apartments after that with a sequence of friends and
lovers, he went to sleep on the couch. The cats came to cuddle
on his chest and belly, but soon curled up against the sofa's back
cushion. The two small creatures snored loudly enough to wake
him once, and when he moved they started purring, as if to
persuade him to remain still.

When the alarm on the phone rang, he got up and dressed in
the clothes he had arrived in. In the kitchen he opened the food
cabinet and saw that most of the cans were still there. Beanie
avoided processed food as much as she could and usually made
her meals from scratch. He put a few tins of tomato paste, crab
meat, pineapple, and mushrooms in the backpack. Most of his
winter clothes were in the cabin, but he took out a wool sweater
and a good shirt and pants from the bedroom closet, rolled

them up, and put them inside a plastic bag to protect them in the backpack. He left a "Goodbye I love you all will mail soon" note to Beanie on the kitchen worktop and petted the cats in turn. Then he exited the apartment and locked the door behind him.

The elevator was empty and silent. In the mirror on the rear wall he was a tall, lean shape in a blue mountain jacket and gray cargo pants. The empty foyer smelled of cigarettes and stale air from the entrance. He entered the cold December drizzle, the almost deserted parking lot, and the bare lindens outside. The morning was quiet, carrying the scent of wood smoke, fog, and bone meal from the feed factory in the bay. The tiny droplets that hung in the air felt like cold kisses. On the path through the narrow park that led from the honeycomb towers to the train station he only passed a few dog walkers and some stragglers on their way home from the night's festivities.

He had memorized the time-table before he left the cabin and knew the trains started at ten in the morning after Christmas. He hoped the information was still correct and that the schedule had not been changed over the holiday. The information booths were closed and the only way to check the time tables and buy a ticket was via the monitors and vending machines that were clustered inside the station.

He had to wait for less than fifteen minutes before the train arrived and when it did it was just a couple of minutes late. Only a handful of people exited the compartments, pulling large suitcases or carrying tall backpacks, and even fewer passengers boarded. This time, there was plenty of space for his luggage on the shelf inside the car, and most of the seats were empty. He almost called Michael to say goodbye, but he assumed Michael had been up late the night before, and sent a message instead, saying that he loved him and thought of him all the time, and that he was welcome to visit the cabin any time.

The journey back to the mountains was obscured by fog and rain. The bilberry and heather that were visible along the tracks were almost bare, and the trees and bushes looked as if they'd never grow leaves again. But when he came down the path to the cabin, the last rays from the pale winter sun, as it sank in flames behind the mountains, revealed that green stalks were jutting all over the heath.

27

HE WAS DETERMINED TO BE AS WELL PREPARED for the upcoming tests as he possibly could. During the time that remained before the meeting he ran for several hours daily, along the fields if the ground was dry, or on the treadmill on the terrace if the soil was too wet. For strength he did exercises that utilized his own body weight, a variety of push-ups, pull-ups, sit-ups, squats, dips, and kicks.

In the morning and midday, when he was most alert, he cycled through the tests he had taken for the first round of the application, and searched for similar tests online. He suspected he had to have as few errors as possible on the tests, and at the same time do them as quickly as possible, to have a chance to pass. He assumed he would be compared with not only a statistical population average, but also against the other applicants. He didn't know how many or how experienced they would be, but assumed that in addition to an education in the natural sciences, engineering, or medicine, many of them would also have a military or aviation background, perhaps even as fighter pilots or rescue divers. He wondered how many of them had seen action.

Some days into the new year he took the train past his home city to a larger one further south on the coast, departed at its central station, and from there caught a tram to a quiet campus in the suburbs.

The astronaut training center did not distinguish itself from the surrounding low and rectangular structures which, judging from their logos and signs, housed various science and technology companies and research institutions. Only the large scale models of various launch rockets outside indicated that the building was dedicated to activities in space.

A row of flags whipped in the high winds that the new year always seemed to bring. He pulled the hood of his jacket up and pushed his hands deeper into the pockets. Even here, far south of the mountains, the wind was cold and insistent enough to chill the hardshell outer garment and the fleece jacket beneath. It was one of the few times he had felt truly cold that winter. Above the fluttering flags, dense clouds rushed by, looking heavy with rain or snow. The mid-morning was as gloomy as dusk and unlikely to become much brighter until the meager daylight turned to darkness.

At the entrance of the astronaut training center sat a large model of the space organization's most recent spacecraft, an oblong shape in a matte gray color, with sharp, cutting angles, which made it look as fast and deadly as a shark. He recalled what he had read about the new spacecraft on the organization's web site; the vessel had been in development for more than a decade and had started as an experimental vehicle to test whether a spacecraft with acute angles and flat planes would deflect the heat and pressure of reentry to the Earth's atmosphere better than the traditional ones with rounded shapes. From there the spacecraft had been successful at test after test and was now in use as a transportation and cargo system for astronauts in low orbit. Perhaps a modified, larger version of the spacecraft would be constructed for the journey to the red planet?

The glass doors slid open with a breath of hot air from the heaters above to reduce the chill from outside. He passed an inner set of glass doors and entered a surprisingly small foyer where more models of orbital probes and satellites and other spacecraft were displayed on brushed steel pedestals and in canvas-printed photographs on the walls.

A woman in a white blouse, dark blazer, and dark skirt, was holding a clipboard with the space organization's logo on the back. She welcomed him and asked if he was there for the testing.

He nodded and smiled.

The woman smiled back, her teeth white and even. "Please wait here," she said. "When everyone has arrived I will call you to follow me."

Along the back wall of the foyer was a bench with leather cushions for waiting guests to rest their legs, but he felt too energized to sit down. Instead, he wandered around and took in the many models and pictures and plaques that described the space organization's activities in low Earth orbit, at Mercury, Venus, Mars, Jupiter, Saturn, and the second lagrangian point. The tiles on the floor were made from a black mineral that had tiny, sparkling crystals locked inside, polished to a high shine and a smooth surface. The effect was that of standing in deep space and looking at the multitudes of stars.

When he arrived only a few other candidates dressed in thick winter clothing were waiting in the foyer, but during the next half hour, the room filled with men and women of various ages and builds, so many that he could only study a few of them without staring openly. Some of the arrivals spent the time looking at the exhibits or smiling faintly to everyone else. Others sat down on the bench by the wall, read on their phones or books or newspapers they had brought with them. One or two were eating a packed breakfast. As far as he could see there were about fifty people in the room when the space organization's representative stepped in the middle of the floor and asked for their attention.

"Welcome everyone!" she smiled. "So happy to see you could make it to the testing today and found your way here. I hope you all had a good journey. Please follow me, and we'll get started right away."

The small crowd picked up their belongings and followed the representative through a doorway in the back of the foyer, down a corridor with a mezzanine and skylights in the ceiling. Beneath the skylights hung a series of transparent plastic banners in the sequential colors of the rainbow, each displaying the logo of a former space mission, emitting a full spectrum of colors on the blank white walls. The group was upbeat, but quiet as they passed beneath the rainbow-colored light on the starry floor.

Further in, the hallways of the training center became darker and narrower than those they had followed from the foyer. The space organization's representative took them down a long corridor, then a shorter one, and finally into a spacious room supplied with rows of desks and computer monitors.

"Please find a seat," the representative said. "There should be more than enough room for everyone."

When the group had settled, the representative called their names one by one from the sheet on her clipboard. As each person answered, the group turned toward them with curious looks, like a class of students meeting for the first time. At first he tried to memorize the names and faces, but gave up when it became clear that there were too many people to remember without knowing something more about them to use as a mnemonic. Most of the prospective astronauts seemed to be in their late twenties to early forties, with a few younger and several older, and seemed to come from all over the continent.

He remembered what Katsuhiro had said when he told him about the medical certificate necessary for the testing.

"Isn't that a little ableist?" Katsuhiro said. "No handicapped, ill, or slow people need apply, no glasses, asthma, or rheumatism in space. I'm surprised they allow women, gay, and people of color."

"Space is sadly not accessible for everyone yet," he had replied. "Only for the able-bodied or the extremely rich."

"Yes, as I said," Katsuhiro finished.

Now he recalled his brother's words, but none of the candidates looked super-human; they seemed like people he saw every day in the city.

After the roll call the space organization's representative asked them to turn on the computers at their desks. A few candidates couldn't find the switches and had to glance at the others to see where they were placed.

"Is this the first test?" someone asked loudly, and everyone laughed, even the representative.

"When you have all turned on your computers, please click our logo in the upper left corner of the screen," the representative said. "Then start by filling out your name, date of birth, and address, and choose 'send.' After that you may start the first test when you are ready to begin. This test is in our intranet only, but will be timed and look quite similar to what you have completed earlier online. We're testing you electronically and individually for easier and faster scoring."

28

ALTHOUGH THE TESTS RESEMBLED THE ONLINE versions, they were longer and more complex, and the time to answer them was shorter. As before, attention, memory, perception, and intelligence were tested, with the addition of basic mathematics and engineering. He added and subtracted, divided and multiplied, predicted the next symbol in the sequence, read black and white dials, and memorized colors and patterns. After a few challenging hours during which the only sounds in the large room full of people was the clattering of keyboards and the clicking of mice, the representative asked them to finish up the test and follow her to the cafeteria in fifteen minutes.

"Please leave your bags," the representative said when the break started. "They are perfectly safe here. I will hand you tickets for lunch, but any extra beverage you must pay for yourselves, so do bring money if you would like something extra to drink."

A few people muttered under their breath, but joined in the rest of the group as they rummaged in bags and wallets after payment.

The representative led them through more corridors to what looked like the main thoroughfare of the building, a long and wide hallway with a lot of traffic, their footfalls and voices filling its space. From here smaller corridors branched off to more peripheral parts of the facility, the openings interspersed with narrow floor-to-ceiling windows which looked out on the winter-stripped garden and the gray clouds outside. Lining the corridor's interior wall were display cases and miniature exhibitions. The main hallway ended in a circular atrium filled with chairs and tables and potted indoor trees beneath wide skylights. Along the wall stood a row of counters with stacked trays and plates, cutlery in plastic cases, bread in baskets, cereals in bowls, bottles of soda, beer, and wine, jugs of coffee and hot water for tea, juice in dispensers, jams, lunch meats, mixed salads and fresh fruits in chilled bowls, and steaming pots and pans with a variety of soups, fried fish, baked vegetables, and grilled meat.

The space organization's representative handed out meal tickets to the group and the candidates lined up by the counters. Some of them were already talking with each other; perhaps they were from the same city, work place, university, or organization.

He chose a generous helping of fried salmon, baby asparagus, green salad, and ice water, loaded the plates up on his tray and carried it to the counter.

"Any extra beverage?" the employee behind the till said as she took his lunch ticket.

He shook his head, took his tray, and started looking for the other candidates. A sizeable group of them occupied one of the largest tables in the dining area, by a window facing the garden.

"Is it taken?" he asked the woman at the end of the table.

"No, please join us," she said and smiled.

More candidates arrived at the table and the small talk started up. As expected in a group of strangers, the chat consisted mostly of introductions, talk of home city, job, education, but also why they had applied to the program. After a short while the conversations were surprisingly easy for a large group of people that had never met before. They already had several things in common, not just the two previous rounds of tests. Most had been interested in space science and exploration from an early age, and had pursued their education and job opportunities accordingly.

"I love science and know how challenging exploring space is, but I also call myself a space romantic and will always be one," the oldest of the candidates said, a tall man with a thinning hairline who worked as a teacher and journalist.

"Me too," several others said and laughed, clearly identifying with the description. There were too many names to remember, but he already recognized several of the candidates by their faces or clothes.

"What happened with the project that planned to land people on Mars as a one-way trip?" someone said.

"They had a website to apply at, but there were rumors that you had to donate to the program to be considered for selection. After the finalists were picked, there was no more news about the project."

"Did they go bankrupt?" someone asked. That had been the fate for numerous companies in the current economic downturn, which seemed to have no end.

"They were probably a scam from the start. They claimed they were sending people to Mars, but had no spacecraft, no solutions for radiation and nutrition, no habitat modules, and no scientific experiments, or backing."

"That's reassuring," another candidate said.

Laughter rippled through the group.

"How about the astronaut training program on the eastern continent that was broadcast as a reality show?"

"I think they ended up with three or four candidates who are still waiting to be launched," another said. "No idea to where."

"Best to go with someone who's actually sent people into space before," someone else remarked, to more chuckles from the others.

29

IN HIS DREAMS HE WATCHED THE FULL MOON
flare like a star, licking the sky with long protuberances that died
down momentarily to cascade new lunar ejections. The moon
flares pulled at him like magnetism, crackled on his skin like
electricity, and burned like the sun.

Cosmic radiation, he thought and scrambled like a rodent to
find shelter, anywhere, everywhere. While he scuttled along a
barren stone plain, a helicopter veered into the radius of the
searing tongues in the firmament, the aircraft black and silhouetted against the glare of the raging moon, and exploded in a
plume of fire, the rotor blades and fuselage dissolving, melting,
dripping to the ground.

He kept fleeing from the cosmic radiation, and then Michael
was there, inviting him home. He suspected that Michael was
still hurt by his unfaithfulness and moving to the cabin, but he
pretended not to notice and followed Michael down to the basement. There, Michael's parents were waiting for them. Michael
handed him a folded note ruled in blue, like a school notebook.
The note displayed Michael's phone number in black ink. He
stared at the digits, but they were blurry and morphed fluidly

into other numbers, even when he folded the note and opened it again for closer inspection.

Michael then showed him pages of a comic book story he had been working on, and with visible pride handed him sheet after sheet of drawn panels. He didn't know Michael could draw, or even that he liked comic books, and took in the artwork with surprise. The pages were as mutable and fuzzy as the phone number on the note, but he squinted and rotated the sheets to make as much sense of them as possible. His skin still burned so he knew they weren't safe, but he hoped the lunar rays were like alpha radiation, as long as they had something thicker than a sheet of paper between them and the source, the damage was reduced.

The fluid, metamorphosing panels of Michael's artwork contained black and white drawings of city buildings, a leafless forest, a blank sky, and tiny figures that were searching for something that was just around the corner from them, behind nearby trees, or beneath the gravel on the ground. The characters were so small he couldn't make out their faces or tell them apart, and although he tried to grasp the story by reading the panels over and over, they shifted and changed like the lunar flares, and he was at a loss of understanding what the story was about.

"It's wonderful," he lied, "thank you for showing it to me," and handed the sheets back to Michael.

Michael was smiling broadly, looking boundlessly happy, as if he had asked him for marriage. Above them the air rumbled and shrieked as the rays from the moon pierced the heavens and the roof and their flesh.

He woke in the hotel room the space organization had billeted them in. Sweating, he threw the lumpy duvet aside, but did not get up to avoid disturbing the candidate who slept in the bed on the other side of the room. Even through the curtains the windows were pale and gray. With the hotel being situated by the sea, the management had apparently chosen diaphanous fabrics and sunny dawns to double-lined drapery and darkness for restful sleep. The sun was still not up, but close.

The previous day the tests had continued until five in the afternoon, then the space organization's representative had taken them back to the foyer with the star-gleaming floor. A large coach had pulled up outside the front and taken them to one of the many hotels along the beach outside the city center. It had been dark when they arrived, but the fifteen-floor building was lit by orange floodlights and stood like a shining pillar among the grass-tufted dunes. Less than twenty meters from the broad stairs and entrance, which were also flooded with orange light, the ocean rolled slow waves ashore, and the smell of the sea and the sand granted a fleeting illusion of summer.

In the reception and in the restaurant at dinner they encountered only a few other guests, two middle-aged couples traveling together, a small group of senior citizens on tour with a guide, and a cluster of visitors from the western continent who talked loudly and laughed even louder, and left the next morning in two minibuses. Other than them the hotel was cold and empty and seemed to be waiting quietly for warmer weather and busier times.

30

ON THE SECOND DAY AT THE ASTRONAUT TRAIN-
ing center he was prepared for more mathematical, perception,
attention, and intelligence tests, but when the candidates were
gathered in the small foyer in the morning, the representative
informed them that the time would be used for medical and
psychological tests. Some in the group exchanged glances.

As the previous day, the representative led them past the hallway with the mezzanine and spectrum of banners, through the
narrow corridors, to the room with the desks and the monitors.
There she presented them with the tasks at hand:

"Today we will be asking you questions about your past and
present health, and also the health of your closest family members in order to rule out certain hereditary diseases. These questions may feel uncomfortable and you are not obliged to fill out
the form, but unless we know a little bit about you and your
family's medical history, it will be very difficult to assess you."

"You may refuse to answer the questions, but it'll cost you the
spot in the program," one candidate muttered.

"These tests are not timed so you may leave for small breaks
or lunch whenever you wish," the representative continued. "I
recommend that you save your progress in the tests so you don't

lose any data during the break. Good luck, everyone, and feel free to ask if you have any questions."

The first document was a medical questionnaire where he filled out his name, address, phone number, email address, and birth date. He then ticked boxes to answer whether he had undergone recent surgery and for what illness or injury, if he had any chronic diseases or allergies and describe them, whether he had had any serious illnesses such as cancer, stroke, or heart problems as a teenager or as an adult, and what infectious and other diseases and health issues he had experienced as a child. He typed, "broken fingers, right hand," for recent surgery, and ticked off none for chronic diseases, as well as chickenpox, influenza, middle ear infection, and colds under childhood ailments, and colds for adult infectious diseases. The questionnaire reminded him of those he had filled out for his military service and health insurance, but were more exhaustive and took longer to complete.

"Let's hope this test stays with the space organization," one of the candidates behind him murmured.

"I was just thinking the same thing," the person next to her replied.

The second questionnaire was even more detailed and invasive. It contained almost the same categories and questions as the first test, but this time pertaining to his immediate family: parents, siblings, and children. Even grandparents were included in the list.

"Are they really allowed to ask about our families' health?" one candidate said so loudly everyone could hear it. The representative had left them to the tests. "It's not like we're inbred or anything."

"This is not just about present diseases," another candidate replied. "Common health issues like diabetes and certain cancers also have a large hereditary component to them, and they want to know how likely we are to develop those in the future."

"I'm not going to tell them anything," a third person said. "I have no right to give out detailed information about other people's health." Several candidates expressed their agreement.

He started to fill out the form, slowly and hesitantly, and not only because he wasn't certain what diseases his brother had had when they were small, and even less so his parents, but whether he really ought to report on the health of his family without their consent. If he lied, or pretended that he didn't know or remember what diseases the members of his family had contracted in the past, would the space organization track down the correct information from medical records anyway?

He simply didn't know, so he filled out the form for his family's medical history as correctly, but also as vaguely, as he could. Sprained thumb, chickenpox, mumps, influenza, and cold he ticked off for his younger brother. As far as he knew and could remember none of his immediate family had suffered any serious diseases or injuries when they grew up, and if they currently did, they hadn't told him about it. For his parents he could only fill out influenza and cold as he assumed they had experienced that as children, but he didn't know of anything more. He was even less familiar with the health status of his grandparents in the past, but ticked high blood pressure for his maternal grandfather and type two diabetes for his paternal grandmother.

After that followed detailed questionnaires about his mental health and that of his family. These documents listed a host of mental illnesses, from depression to schizophrenia, including phobias he'd never heard of, and he didn't tick any of them. Finally, he started on a series of psychological examinations. The first test mapped the five main components of personality: extraversion, openness to experience, conscientiousness, agreeableness, and neuroticism. Since he had been through a similar psychological evaluation in the military, he assumed there would also be interviews with psychologists, probably for those who passed the current round of tests. He answered the personality questionnaire as truthfully, but also as favorably, as he could.

The second questionnaire reminded him of certain personality tests he had taken online for fun, but it contained more questions, many of them repeated or rephrased, and seemed to go into much more detail than the simple tests found on the internet. He assumed the space organization wanted to know as much as possible about the candidates' personality types and psychological profiles. His responses to those kinds of personality tests hadn't changed much since he first started taking them for fun online, and now he gave the same answers as he always did.

The last portion he also recognized from personality tests online, but again it was a more advanced and detailed version. This test mapped possible personality disorders or other psychological issues. As with the mental health questionnaire, it contained a long list of phobias, this time accompanied by a short explanation. Was he afraid of heights, confined spaces, the sight of blood, going to the dentist, going to the doctor, spiders, insects, hair, water, or fire? Did he feel the need to check whether he had locked the door, switched off the stove, or pulled out the electrical cords twice or more in a row? Was he compelled to wash his hands for more than five minutes, to shower or bathe more than twice a day, to not step on cracks on the sidewalk, or count things repeatedly? How often did he drink, smoke, gamble, take illegal drugs, or purchase sex (including the use of pornography) per week?

Thinking it might look odd if he didn't tick any of the phobias, he checked spiders. There would probably be few arachnids in space, except for lab specimens. For the addictions he typed in numbers befitting a monk or someone who lived alone in the mountains.

31

ON THE THIRD DAY OF TESTING THE CANDIDATES
were called out of the meeting room in groups of three for a
medical examination. While the others waited their turn, they
continued to fill out any unfinished forms from the previous
day.

A few doors down the hallway from the meeting room, a
team of three doctors, two men and a woman in white coats,
were waiting in a large space with three desks, three examination
benches, and three exercise bikes wired to a rack of monitors.
The winter sun blazed in through wide arched windows, the
intense illumination barely dampened by translucent curtains.
The room smelled faintly of disinfectant and soap.

He and the other candidates started by signing a form which
allowed the doctors to perform various medical and dental tests
and that they consented to not being informed of the general
results, unless the analyses indicated actual disease. He signed
the document thinking that if he didn't pass the current round
of selection, he'd at least had a free and thorough health check.
The doctor he had been assigned took his pulse and blood pressure, examined his heart and lungs with a stethoscope, looked
inside his eyes, ears, mouth, and throat, measured and noted his

height, weight, and percentage of body fat, and examined his spine and shoulders. Then followed several blood tests taken from his arm in small plastic tubes, and a urine sample, which he had to obtain in the bathroom next door and hand to the doctor in a small, closed cup. In the adjacent room, a general x-ray was taken of his chest and abdomen and another of his head and neck. Back in the large room, the doctor glued electrodes to his chest and neck and wrists and told him to lie down on the nearest examination bench to measure his heart function and rate at rest. After that he had to put on a nose clip and a breathing mask, which sent signals to the rack of monitors and consoles in the corner, and mount one of the exercise bikes to measure lung capacity and heart output during moderate exercise and at full load. He was very glad he had been training the entire fall, and was relieved when it took a while for his pulse to reach maximum rate during the final test. Finally, he had to go two doors down the hallway for a full x-ray of his mouth and teeth, and check-up with a dentist.

He had expected even more invasive medical tests, but they were probably more costly and might therefore not happen until the final round of selection. When the candidates returned to the hotel it was almost dark. That close to the sea the dusk turned blue before it fell to black, and large, wet flakes of sleet wafted down into the slowly beating waves.

At dinner the atmosphere was quiet and subdued, despite most of the fifty candidates being present and filling nearly all of the small white-clothed tables in the hotel's restaurant. It was as if their chatter and laughter dissipated into a vacuum beneath the high, molded ceiling and the mint-green walls decorated with naturalist drawings of local plant species. In the draft from the tall, narrow windows the meticulously prepared dishes cooled too quickly, and the light from the multi-colored blown-glass chandeliers from the southern parts of the continent seemed much too bright. The sound of the waves that hissed ashore slowed their hearts and stilled their thoughts. For a while the only noises in the room were the clink of silverware against porcelain, the scraping of chairs as someone sat down by a table or left one, and the waiters' footsteps on the shiny, lacquered floor.

"Seems it's getting colder tonight," one candidate said, breaking the chilled silence.

"That's the problem with January," another candidate replied. "After Christmas and New Year's there's nothing to look forward to except spring, and that never arrives fast enough." There was a flurry of laughter in agreement, then nothing but cutlery against plates was heard for a good while.

He attributed the silence to people being hungry and sleepy after three days of testing, and in particular, the exercise load of the medical examination. His own legs were sore after the biking, because he hadn't dared take the time to warm up before going on the bike, or stretch properly when it was done. He had wanted to, but it had seemed so self-important and delaying, especially since neither of the other two candidates testing at the same time had warmed up or stretched. Now feeling the minor but definite pain in his thighs and calves, he regretted not having asked for the time after all.

"I wonder what they're going to put us through tomorrow," someone muttered.

"I'd rather like to know which of us are going to the next round," another replied.

"You think they've already made their choices?" a third said.

"Yes, of course, don't be naive."

"Isn't it always so? There may be ten suitable applicants for a position, but the leadership has already decided, even if the position is advertised publicly."

"And if not, then there's always one or two who stand out right from the start and the others haven't really got a chance."

The candidates glanced around, some more openly than

others, to find out who might be familiar to the space organization already, or had distinguished themselves during the tests, but since, with the exception of the medical examinations, all the testing had been done electronically and without adjudicators, no one had any facts to base their considerations on, and consisted only of impressions and guesses.

He wondered too, but shifted his focus back on the sole of halibut in morel and sweet wine sauce on his plate, cutting it deliberately, and chewing even more slowly.

"You can't mean that," one candidate finally said. "They wouldn't have invited all of us here and paid for the tests and the hotel if just a handful of us were proper astronaut material."

"Take it easy," another replied. "This isn't a talent show on TV. They will have to analyze and compare the tests first; it'll take them weeks at least, or even months."

"No, the representative told me herself this morning who would be called in for the next round of tests."

Silence, then laughter, incredulous, yet a little nervous.

"That's rubbish."

More laughter around the tables.

Cut, skewer, swish, chew. Fingers getting cold and thighs aching on the seat of the chair. Draft from the windows chilled the back of his neck.

"I suppose you're right. It will take them weeks to sort through the data. But think about it, each of us might be looking at their crew mates to the moon, or even to Mars!"

They looked at one another.

Someone snickered, high and thin, but quickly fell silent.

32

AFTER THE SUBDUED DINNER HE EXPECTED A
mass retreat to the rooms, but instead most of the candidates
gathered in the hotel bar, clearly seeking the warmth of human
company and friendly conversation from the deep leather chairs
around the crackling fireplace, while the heads of several unfor-
tunate ungulates glared at them from the hunting lodge decor
on the walls. The rest of the applicants huddled on the roof-
covered steps at the main entrance, sending the stench of cigarettes and snippets of talk into the foyer every time someone
moved too close to the doors and made them slide open.

He sat for a while in the bar, chatting with a few of the other
candidates while ordering peanuts and salt sticks instead of
drinks, then excused himself early.

"I'm going upstairs," he told his roommate, Wameeth, an
outgoing, broad-shouldered father of two who hailed from the
northeastern region of the southern continent.

"Not staying longer?" Wameeth said. "It's the last night after
all."

He shook his head. "I'm worn out. But please stay for as long
as you'd like."

"All right, see you later, my friend."

Upstairs in the room he turned off the lamps, pulled the thin curtains aside, and pushed the nearest windows open. Wet snow flakes speckled the air and dusted the garden and driveway with white, but didn't seem cold enough to remain. He thought he could hear the snowflakes hiss as they reached the black surface of the water and melted into it, but he could neither see nor hear the surf.

When it grew too cold, he shut the window and went to bed. Before the testing started, he had worried about the white light and wondered if it would flare up in him, but the white-outs had stayed away, perhaps because he spent all his mental and physical energy on the tests. Thus, instead of collapsing from seizures, he stopped breathing in his sleep. He couldn't say what he was thinking of or dreaming about when it happened, only that he woke up because he couldn't remember the last time he had felt his body draw breath. It was a surprising and strange sensation, but not one that elicited fear. When it happened, it felt natural and appropriate, something that simply should be allowed to take place without his interference or opinion, just like the white light and the sensation he had had in the summer of vanishing into it. He had read that some experienced practitioners only needed to draw their breath once or twice an hour, deep in meditation. Since the silence that preceded and followed the spontaneous breath-hold was meditative and calming, he assumed he was experiencing something similar.

He expected to fall asleep quickly, but that didn't happen. Despite the feeling of exhaustion, he lay staring into the darkness while listening to the clangs of the elevator further down the hallway as it started and stopped, footsteps in the corridor, muted sounds from the floor above, water gurgling in the pipes. An hour later he was roused from a light sleep by the sound of laughter right outside the door and voices he thought he recognized. The last disturbance before he fell solidly into dreams was that of Wameeth opening the door from the lit hallway and then closing it quickly.

The next morning he rose as soon as the alarm clock integrated in the headboard of the bed rang, had a quick shower, shaved, dressed, then packed his small backpack and carried it downstairs to the luggage room in the reception. The space organization representative had informed them that their rooms would be paid, but that they had to check out themselves, so that the hotel could confirm how many of the reserved rooms had been used. He did so at the front desk and handed his key in before he entered the restaurant for breakfast. As with the previous mornings, there were no warm dishes, not even porridge, but instead, a wide variety of cereals, bread, sliced meat, jams, fruits and vegetables, and steaming coffee and tea, which had been set out on a long table in front of the windows. He took a plate and a glass from the stacks at the head of the buffet and helped himself to some rye bread, smoked ham, red chili, and mini cucumber.

Outside, the lawn and hedges that lay in shadow were covered in a spotty layer of wet snow, but where the sun's rays had reached the vegetation was bare and the rest would likely melt long before noon. The sky was bright and the ocean a clear, calm blue. It looked like a beautiful day in the beginning of spring instead of in the winter. He hoped the fields at the cabin were growing fast and well.

After breakfast, the chartered coach that had shuttled them the previous days took them to the astronaut training center for the last time. Now familiar with the building, the candidates rolled their suitcases, carried their backpacks, and lugged their bags through the hallways to the large meeting room.

"Today you have until lunch to finish up and revise any test that you haven't yet completed," the space organization's representative said. "If for some reason you need more time to finalize all your tests, let me know and I will see what I can do. Those of you who wish to leave earlier for the journey home may do so, but please notify me before you go so I know you have left and aren't simply missing."

Most of the candidates had only parts of a test or two to complete, and a few left within the hour. But the majority seemed to have scheduled their return trips to the afternoon and said they preferred waiting at the astronaut training center than at the airport or the train station. One of them collected their names, email addresses, and internet profiles, and promised to set up a group online for those who wished to stay in touch.

The candidates who had completed their tests drifted off to the cafeteria for a bite to eat. The representative said she couldn't offer them food tickets that day, but that the prices in the cafeteria were highly subsidized, so she recommended buying lunch there before they left.

Several of the candidates, especially those who lived near one another, or had attended the same university, or had been stationed at the same military base, exchanged personal addresses and phone numbers. The week of testing seemed to have resulted in several new friendships and a few romantic connections. He gave his email address to a few others, including Wameeth, without expecting to hear much from them, but nevertheless looked forward to chatting with them as part of the group online.

During their final lunch together in the cafeteria the candidates also organized shared transport to the airport and the train station. When the meal was over they picked up their luggage in the meeting room, and followed the representative one last time to the foyer.

"Best of luck to everyone and I hope to see you again for the next and final round of selections," the representative said, smiling at them. "It's been such a pleasure to meet you all and to get to know our future explorers."

He traveled with the smallest group, which was headed to the central train station.

"Looking forward to going back to the mountains?" Wameeth asked.

"Yes," he said. "Are you familiar with the place?"

"Passed through it once or twice on the way to my company's ski cabin. It's a beautiful place, but cold."

"It's gotten warmer," he said. "It's still beautiful, though."

"Warmer?" Wameeth said. "Isn't there a lot of snow?"

"No snow so far," he said, "but it's my first season there, so it might just be the strange weather this year."

"Yes, the weather has been so weird," Wameeth said. "I wonder when it's going to turn back to normal. When I heard you lived up there I thought you were staying at the resorts."

"No," he smiled. He hadn't seen any ski slopes or hotels. They must be further up in the mountains.

"So you're not a ski bum? Why do you live there then?"

"I bought a cabin," he said.

"And then the snow disappears. Isn't that typical?"

"Yes," he laughed and avoided mentioning that snow had had nothing to do with his moving there.

By the time he stepped onto the platform on the moor and started on the path to the cabin, it had been dark for hours and he had to put on his headlamp before he entered the heath. The densely quiet darkness closed around him and almost swallowed the faint beam. He imagined that he was traversing the bottom of the deep sea or the surface of a barren, distant world.

33

AFTER FOUR DAYS SURROUNDED BY PEOPLE, COM-
ing back to the cabin was strange. He had expected that being
among so many people would be hard after a long time in the
mountains, but it seemed instead that it was solitary existence
which required acclimatization. Clearly, humans were pack animals, not soloists like octopi, or even social by circumstance like
tigers seemed to be, but true pack animals that not only wanted,
but needed to be social. He'd read somewhere that if a person
grew up without interacting with other people, she or he would
not become a true human being, and lack language, empathy, and
all other forms of social skills. He wondered about that. Kaye
had said that empathy, the ability to sympathize with and care
for another being, preceded humans, was older than humanity
itself. It was a trait shared by many mammals, might even be the
characteristic that defined mammalian behavior, caused by the
need to rear the young for a long while, and to do it with great
care, often inside a complex social structure.

"Did empathy evolve to strengthen the social structure, or
was social structure a result of the empathy that evolved?" he
had asked the assistant professor once.

"That, I nor anyone else can say with certainty," Kaye said, smiling. "We don't know which appeared first, empathy or complex social structure, perhaps they did so simultaneously. But after they first appeared, each affected the evolution of the other greatly, and today they may be inseparable."

The silence in the cabin was interrupted only by the occasional whistle of wind from beneath the door, the gurgle of water when he opened the tap in the kitchen, and the crackling of fire as the logs burned in the hearth. The quiet filled his ears the same way the newly fallen snow had dampened all sounds in the restaurant at the last dinner during the testing. He welcomed the stillness and sat inside it while the residue of the other candidates' presences and voices, the sights and smells of the past week, played themselves out in his mind and slowly faded.

As he had expected, it had been difficult to sleep well in a shared room, not to mention shared with someone who snored loudly for most of the night. The energy required to answer the tests accurately and quickly, to keep abreast of the multiple conversations that had been going on around him, and to connect the right names to the correct faces, had been considerable. The first night back in the cabin he slept for twelve hours, and for ten hours on the second night.

In his dreams he met Eloise and half expected her to provide him with a progress report about the project. Instead, he found himself describing a place high up in the mountains for her. As he did so, he remembered the site from earlier dreams and what he had done there the previous times. It was one of his recurring dream-places, although he rarely felt the need to see it again. But now the memory of that imaginary landscape pulled at him, even inside the ongoing dream, and he realized why he kept returning to it, like a bird on oneiric migration.

"Take the train north to the highest stop, cross the road, follow the trail past the houses and the grove, and you're there," he said. But as he registered his own words, he felt a sting of regret for having revealed the information of how to reach the location to someone else, even just the dream-representation of another person. He also recalled how worried he had been the first time he discovered the still, dark face of the lake, and the barren, crater-like sides that grew steeply out of it and rose to jagged crags. It was like the fountain in the park, a place in his dreams which upon discovery revealed itself as an often visited, but hidden memory. Perhaps that was what made the lake frightening: uncovering a recurring, but forgotten dream-location, and wondering how many more existed in his subconscious which he couldn't remember.

"I can't go there alone," the dream version of Eloise said, looking too concerned and insecure to be the person he knew from his waking hours.

"It's not that far," he said, but agreed to visit the lake with her, as he yearned to see it himself.

He wasn't certain when he last dreamed about the place, six months ago, a year, two years, but the journey there was more or less how he remembered it. A small train, its compartments more reminiscent of a funicular or a trolley in a city, climbed slowly upward. As the train ascended, the landscape changed abruptly from plains to mountains. One moment the windows were black, the next they were filled with tall white peaks.

Eloise and he disembarked at an empty platform by the road, where the rail tracks continued to who knew where in his dreaming mind. Then they followed the road which wound through the pass uphill and around a curve. There, on the other side of the narrow strip of asphalt was a parking lot, and above it a pale wooden building with unusual angles and a ribbed steel roof. That was the local tourist center, where he had bought stickers and key rings in earlier dreams. But this time they walked in the opposite direction, to a cluster of houses nestled in the mountain side, private homes which looked surprisingly suburban, surrounded by lawns and flowering hedges. His dream view tilted like a camera, revealing a bright, warm sun in the sky. That had not happened before; during his earlier visits it had been dusk or winter.

The lake was where he recalled it, its precipitous sides and looming cliffs the same as in earlier dreams. But when Eloise and he descended the graveled slope and reached the edge of the water, the lake had dried up and all that was left was an expanse of black mud.

"My god, where have all the fish gone?" Eloise said.

"They are still here," he replied, sensing the trout and pike and eel and perch buried in the dark substrate. "See?" He plunged his hands into the silt. Beneath the dusty surface it was still moist and cold. He was soiled up to his elbows, but felt scale-covered bodies wriggle just beneath his fingers.

The lake was gone, somehow drained and dried from his dreams. Who knew if the lake would return to its former state or whether, once changed, dream-locations stayed that way. He wanted to howl in sadness for the loss of the lake and the fish, but said nothing, rose, and took in the gray peaks above them. Now, with the liquid vanished, he felt the way he always did at the shore of the dream-lake, and until then, had forgotten; electricity crackled up his spine like a lightning rod, and a sensation of intense magnetism pulled at him from the surrounding crags.

Despite Eloise, despite the presence of someone else, he did for the first time what he had always wanted to do there: give in to the magnetic sensation and let the electricity run through him while he fell to the ground, flopping like a fish on land. The water in the lake might not return, but it was the cliffs that had pulled him there, not the liquid, as he had thought when the lake had been covered with golden autumn leaves or black winter ice. Even with the water gone, the stone remained unchanged. As he lay seizing on the empty lake bed he remembered that the bodies of water which slept deep beneath the ice in the Antarctic regularly drained and refilled with time.

34

SEVERAL DAYS AFTER HE RETURNED FROM THE astronaut testing, the phone rang. He sat up, feeling a little moist as he always did in the sleeping bag's nylon shell, and felt about for the object that was beeping and buzzing on the floor.

"Yes," he said into the phone, expecting the voice of his brother or Michael.

"Meet me at the Plaza Shopping Center on the coast, tomorrow at eighteen thirty," Kaye said. "It's a private meeting, so don't bring anyone else. And leave your mobile phone at home. I'll be on time so there will be no need to call me."

"All right," he said, puzzled by the immediacy and exactness of the request, but seeing no reason not to do as Kaye wanted. "I'll be punctual as well."

Kaye hung up.

The time until he could see Kaye again passed slowly. He wanted to push at it to go faster, but there was also a pit of apprehension in his stomach. Indoors, the air smelled metallic, and the water from the well tasted of marsh.

By the time he left the cabin it was raining heavily and thunder rumbled in the distance, but the wind was gentle, so he brought the umbrella with him. Beneath its black shield, he took in the fields at both sides of the path. The slim wheat tillers now grew upright, making the moor look more like a wild meadow than a field. The sight made his heart jump and he laughed with joy, momentarily forgetting the trepidation that had been seething in him like an illness.

Once, when his family had traveled to his father's country and the rural town where his grandparents lived, his grandfather had been late to meet them at the station. From far away they had seen an umbrella move toward them on the road between the fields, the color of the fabric and the rhythm of the gait easily recognizable as that of their relative. Then, as now, the umbrella had been black and the fields green on brown.

He caught a train to one of the larger cities on the coast which was nevertheless closer than the seaside resort he had gone to earlier. From there he took a bus to that population center's extensive suburbs, and a massive shopping center with a wide food court and an anonymous cafe which served coffee and a long list of other caffeinated drinks, hot chocolate, soda, mineral water, sandwiches, and slices of cake. Inside the cafe's small refrigerated counter the plastic bottles of water and soft drinks were scratched and matte. The sandwiches were pre-made, wrapped in smeared plastic, bulging with cheese and ham, shrimp and egg salad, and bacon and lettuce slices. The cheese cake, cherry cake, and chocolate cake on offer had been cut into triangles separated by sheets of white paper, the slices looking dry and hard and the paper stained with grease. The cafe claimed only a handful of small round tables and flimsy-looking chairs, separated from the adjacent businesses by dusty wood screens. The open, drafty space stank of the jumble of foods that were being served there, and was filled with the dry, distant sounds of footsteps and voices from the rest of the mall.

He was half an hour early, but didn't settle at the cafe. Instead, he passed the food court and ascended the stairs to the mezzanine above, then followed it back along the second floor while he glanced down at the cafes and restaurants, but saw neither Kaye nor any of the professor's post-docs or graduate students. He entered a wide corridor that led away from the mezzanine and noted the way back. If Kaye had moved to the coast, why did he wish to meet in yet another city? Maybe the professor had found work, or had recently held meetings here?

He scanned the brightly lit, carefully constructed shop exhibits. There was nothing unusual or noteworthy about the shopping center. The stores were neither high end, with designer brands at high prices, nor low end, with nothing but discounted goods, but somewhere safely in the middle. The businesses were a mix of national and international franchises, and what he assumed were local stores, selling clothes, shoes, jewelry, cosmetics, home electronics, garden appliances, children's toys, books, films, music, crafting supplies, groceries, health food, pharmaceuticals, For Her, For Him, For the Children, For the Pet, For the Car, For the Home. A boundless collection of useful and useless objects made from materials that were all finite, but manufactured and sold like they would never cease, marketed to be desired and consumed by as many people as possible, only to be discarded after a few years of use. He suddenly felt sick.

On the way back to the mezzanine he passed a home electronics store displaying a whole wall of TVs of various make and size. All the screens showed the same program: deeply spray-tanned people gaping in mute while they showed off their jeweled watches, brightly colored sports cars, luxury yachts and private jets, and doused one another with sparkling wine from oversized bottles. An on-screen counter registered called-in votes for each participant of the reality show, the numbers turning in the hundreds. Variations in color setting and scan rate made each screen a little different from the rest, some looking orange or delayed, others bluish or slightly blurry, making up a glaring and confusing sight. Nevertheless, his attention was caught by a single monitor in the corner that had been tuned to another channel. At first he thought the image was that of a spiral galaxy viewed head on, the jet from the super-massive black hole in its middle shooting out, like a round from a rifled barrel. But then he realized that the animated vortex which engulfed the meteorological map of the coast was a hurricane, its extreme wind speeds displayed in bruise colors.

When he returned to the cafe in the food court, Kaye was waiting for him at a table as close to the separating screens and as far away from the counter as it was possible to sit. On the silver laminated surface stood two steaming paper cups of coffee.

Kaye lifted one cup in greeting.

He pulled out the other chair at the table and sat down. "You're here for a conference?"

Kaye shook his head. "Just a quick errand. I also thought it would be closer for you to meet here. How are things in the mountains?"

"Good," he said and rose the cup in a reciprocal toast. "Quiet, but good." The hot liquid seared his fingers through the paper, more than warm enough to scald his mouth. He put the cup down without drinking.

Kaye took a sip, then grimaced. "Supposedly, the best coffee comes from beans that have been shat out by a small tropical mammal. Its digestion processes change the beans in a way artificial methods can't. Of course, the animals are now being farmed in battery cages and force-fed coffee beans for commercial purposes."

"That's terrible," he said.

"How is the agricultural project going?" Kaye said.

"Splendid," he said. "The winter wheat has already tillered. It looks as if we shall be able to harvest in the spring."

"Unbelievable," Kaye said.

"How are the lectures going?"

"There's been a lot of interest in them, which is good," Kaye said. "But all of us who are arranging the presentations want to do something more, something concrete, not just talk."

He had intuited as much from Kaye's conviction and secrecy, but had still hoped his suspicions were wrong. Now hearing the assistant professor put it into words made his stomach knot and the skin at the back of his neck feel tight. "Such as?" he finally said.

Kaye leaned closer to him across the table. "The scientists, the policy-makers, and the public have known about the destruction of the environment and the destabilizing of the climate systems for years. The warning signs were there decades ago, but we kept on like it didn't matter. We're paying the price now, all of us. But it's not too late to do something, it's not too late to change."

"It's not?" he muttered.

Kaye's eyes narrowed. "It's never too late to change," Kaye said, meeting his eyes. "But governments will rarely do so, corporations never, not the money, not the power, so we have to do it, we, it's up to us."

Now he understood why the assistant professor's recent life changes looked like a new beginning, or a clean ending. "Why isn't it enough to vote, to elect the right politicians, the right parties?" he said.

"That's what we've been doing for the last decades and look where it's gotten us," Kaye spat. "Another thirty years and we'll still be in the same place, I can guarantee you that."

"So what's the solution, then?" he said, feeling like he was in a spacecraft that was spinning out of control.

"You've utilized your personal initiative for a higher cause before," Kaye said, leaning even closer, breath sour with coffee and the sickening stench of blood on wood wool. "You know what it takes," the assistant professor continued. "A strong mind, clear eyes, steady hands. Why else did you go to the cabin and join that project? How else did you have the stomach to kill the owl?"

This time he simply nodded, but inside he was frantically going over what he had told Kaye about himself, and how much was available online. He had stupidly talked about his service, but how much had he revealed? "I understand," he finally said. "I see the reasons for what you're saying, and I agree with them. But I can't be a part of your plans."

Kaye's face suddenly hardened and his voice lowered to a hiss. "Most people can't do what we're going to. They don't have the skills or the experience, so they don't. But we do, and because of that it is our duty to do it."

"I can't," he said and stood.

He pulled on his jacket with a hard shrug that rattled the keys and the coins in his pockets, and started walking. In the corner of his eye he saw the assistant professor lean back in the hard chair.

"The offer is open," Kaye said calmly behind him. "You have my number."

35

THE HURRICANE REACHED THE CONTINENT A FEW
nights later, its storm front sweeping far inland, even to the
mountains. The precipitation pelted the roof and the walls and
the windows of the cabin, coming from every direction at once,
with no leeward side, no respite, while the wind rattled the old
wood and made it creak and squeak and whistle. The solar-
powered lantern flickered twice in the same hour, then went out
without another warning. To the west the orange light from the
sodium lamp above the door of Eloise and Mark's barn disappeared and the fields lay black before him.

He leaned forward and blew into the birch log that was smoldering in the hearth. Then he closed the powerless laptop, pulled
out the cord in case of lightning, and returned to the sleeping bag on the mattress where he had been lying. The darkness
made the cabin's complaints about the battering from the hurricane louder, even above the roaring of the wind and the gushing
of the rain.

He fell asleep imagining himself a sailor lying in a hammock
in the crew quarters below deck on a tall ship hundreds of years
in the past. In the last moments before the dreams claimed

him, he wondered if the cabin might unmoor itself and start following the rain toward the ocean while he slept.

A loud, persistent noise woke him. He sat up on the mattress, fearing that a part of the roof had been pried loose by the hurricane and was slamming against the rafters, or the storm had gotten hold of a board in the wall and was using it to bang an even larger hole in the wood. But it was neither. Someone was knocking at the door and shining a sharp bluish-white beam through the diamond-shaped window. He was at the door before he registered that he had untangled himself from the sleeping bag, gotten to his feet, and crossed the room. The person outside was shouting his name. He took hold of the door and pulled it open, while he clutched the old handle to prevent the hurricane from yanking the door off its hinges.

Outside were several figures in rain jackets, rain pants, tall rubber boots, and headlamps, reminding him of people wearing hazmat suits. No hardshell fabrics of fancy fibers with chemical waterproofing here, but thick PVC, the same material fishermen's waders and southwesters were made of. His neighbors' faces were hidden by deep hoods and thick scarves. The beams from their trucks and terrain vehicles were as bright as floodlights, yet the thrumming and rumble from the engines was barely audible above the swell of the hurricane. Maybe we're already at sea, he thought, we just don't know it yet.

A face moved close to his to shout over the din of the wind and the engines.

"Come with us, the farms are flooding!" Eloise yelled.

"Where to?" he shouted back. Were they evacuating? That had not been in his plans.

The green-hooded head shook vigorously. "We're not leaving! We're putting out sandbags. We must divert the water from the houses. We need every hand we can get!"

Wool underwear, fleece sweater, the hardshell jacket on top. Running pants covered by the mountaineering pants, the artificial fiber would retain some warmth even if the fabric was rained through. Then knit scarf, knit hat (homemade birthday gifts from Beanie), and leather gloves. Before he left, he scanned the cabin's interior for the safest and sturdiest place. The fridge, it was heavy, solid, and had a rubber seal around the door. He opened it and wedged his phone and wallet behind a packet of organic pork chops and a bag of baby asparagus.

Outside, Eloise directed him to the back of a four-wheel terrain vehicle whose bundled-up driver he recognized as Mark. While he clutched the cargo rack behind him, the storm pushed and buffeted them, stronger than the bouncing and bumping of the vehicle itself as they advanced toward the red buildings of Eloise and Mark's home. The hurricane had already deluged the fields and turned them into a shallow brown sea. Water streamed down the buildings and the sloping courtyard, and had already gouged long tracks in the gravel. By the barn a tractor was rumbling and biting into the earth with its front loader, digging trenches to channel the water from the fields away from the buildings. Behind the trenches, figures in green and orange rain-gear heaved sandbags to raise walls against the flood. Mark stopped at the corner where a mound of sand had been deposited by the wall, and they dismounted.

"Take this!" someone yelled over the storm, holding out a shovel and motioning at some cloth that was shivering on the ground. He took the spade and saw the fabric was empty sacks, for grain or from animal feed, judging by the labels. He squatted down, rolled a bag open, prepared two more, and started filling them with sand. Eloise and Mark joined him, Mark shoveling while Eloise tied the bags together with nylon twine she cut from a large roll with a knife. Other neighbors in the chain stacked the sandbags up around the walls of the house and barn while the tractor continued digging trenches to divert as much water as possible. At the farm to the south, he could see the floodlights of other vehicles, some stationary and others moving about, and knew there was similar frantic activity there. He wondered how Michael and Beanie and his family were, and if the city was being flooded too.

The rain drenched and chilled their faces, the hurricane tore and pushed at them, the engines boomed and thrummed. He shoveled until his fingers became stiff from clutching the spade and his lungs and arms and back felt like they were on fire. When they ran out of sand, they filled the sacks with dirt dug from the trenches. The storm stank of perspiration, diesel fuel, and greasy, waterlogged soil.

Mud and water rushed and swirled into the trenches, creating miniature waterfalls at each downward sloping compartment, then filling the sections that were somewhat level, until the flooding reached to their knees and threatened to sweep away all of the trenches and sandbags. They continued to stanch the flow. When they ran out of bags, they shoveled more channels to lead the water out of those that were already full, shallow troughs that paralleled the first. The hurricane roared and shrieked and rained down with greater intensity, no longer individual gusts but as a ceaseless cascade of water. The deluge soaked every garment and every boot, rubber or not, and if it couldn't penetrate the fabric directly, it seeped in through seams and folds to soak the middle layers and finally drench the skin. The spade handles blistered and the sandbags scoured their hands, whether they wore leather or fabric gloves, and the storm howled like every hungry ghost had been brought to raging, battering life.

It seemed like the rain would never cease, the wind never calm, and the night never end, but then, long after it should have become light, an almost imperceptible brightening of the sky above the summits in the east told them that morning was on its way. Moments later an avalanche of water mixed with pebbles and branches and plants tumbled down the hillock behind the farm. He watched the mudslide and hoped it hadn't been strong enough to push down trees or pull fallen trunks along with it to ram the buildings or the sand walls. The swell surged across the trenches and the sandbags, before it pushed against the pale concrete foundations.

In his early teens he had gone on a class trip to a small lake to collect organisms at its narrow shore: whirligigs, water striders, bowman beetles, snails, toads, and various insect larvae clad in pebble-encrusted tubes. The edge of the lake was covered with vegetation, as thick and dense as a carpet, floating on the water and undulating with it. When he noticed that the plants were solid enough to carry his weight, he fetched a plastic box and a butterfly net, and started out on the floating world, hoping to catch something the other students couldn't.

Unnoticed by the teacher, he moved far along the shore. With each cautious step the floating substrate rose and fell like breath, the sun warmed his face and hands, and the clamor of the others receded in the distance. Soon there was just him and the water and the sound of the tiny flies that hovered in the air. But suddenly the world shifted and he fell until the sky was just a blurry brightness above him, clouded with clumps of vegetation and the bubbles from his own surprised exhalation. The fear of being trapped beneath the plants like someone in the winter would be under ice, shot through him, but he forced himself to relax, hold his breath, and kick hard with his legs. That motion and the air still in his lungs brought him close enough to the surface to bob against the vegetation. Peering up into the brightness and feeling about with his hands, he managed to find the hole he had fallen through, and got his head above water again. From there he pushed his arms and shoulders through the opening and dragged himself up on the billowing surface, heaving and sputtering, reborn from the lake.

He returned far more carefully and humbly than he had left, the box and the net lost beneath the surface. His soaked hair and clothes gained him pointed fingers and loud laughs from his classmates and a stern talking to from the teacher. As punishment he had to shower and then rinse and laundry his clothes in the washing machine in the basement, while the other students marveled at their catches through the magnifying glasses and microscopes in the science lab.

Now he watched the flood with the same fear as when he fell through the hole in the lake, wondering when it would stop and what he should do if it didn't. But the bags and the trenches and the foundations held, the flood slapped against them, before it bubbled and slurped back out into the trenches, and finally the last wave of mud rolled over the brown surface, into the dug furrows, and dispersed. After that less and less water arrived, the day brightened, and the rain almost stopped.

When it was clear the flood had been diverted and someone's radio announced that the storm was finally letting up, the neighbors smiled and cheered and hugged one another.

They stood sweating and trembling inside their soaked-through rain gear, surprised that it was over, uncertain of what to do next.

"Come with us, you can sleep on our couch," Eloise said and touched his shoulder, making him remember the cabin and wonder if it had survived. Was there anything there that couldn't be replaced? He didn't think so.

By foot and by truck they retreated slowly back to the farms and houses. He had no energy left for showering or cleaning, only for hanging up the wet clothing and rubbing his face and hair with a towel, then going to sleep under a large fleece blanket on a sofa that was only a little longer than the three-seater in the cabin.

In the morning there were unstifled yawns and soft padding of feet upon wooden floors and smiles at the table in the kitchen. Somewhere on the farm a generator must be going, providing heat and light, with large pots of drinking water simmering on the stove, ready to be cooled in tall clay jugs with a snippet of parsley for freshness. Breakfast was thick slices of newly defrosted whole-wheat bread, scrambled eggs and bacon, fried sausages, canned herring, pickled cucumber, home-ground mustard, sweet tea, black coffee, and glasses of cooled, boiled water. He ate like it was his last meal.

"We heard on the long-wave band that the hurricane's hit the towns and cities further south so hard the number of dead and injured is still unclear," Eloise said. "The roads are closed, and air and rail travel has been suspended. The phone and internet are also down and millions of homes are without power. It's nearly a complete black-out on the whole coast."

He closed his eyes and thought of Michael, Katsuhiro, and the rest of his family, but said nothing.

"Will you be all right?" Mark asked when he had pulled his still-moist clothes and boots back on and stood in the hallway, ready to leave. "Do you need help with the cabin?"

"I'll be fine," he said, convinced that he would be.

"We'll come by and help you clean up as fast as we can," Eloise said. "We just need to see to the youngest children first."

"Thank you," he said and did not insist on being alone.

The morning was still and quiet, dusted by a thin layer of fog, which softened the cuts and wounds visible from the storm. The flagstones that had lined the flower beds and kitchen garden outside Eloise and Mark's house had been pulled along with the water and strewn out on the pitted, still partly submerged lawn below. Only bits of the garden plants remained, shreds of crocuses, snowdrops, and daffodils, branches of apple and cherry trees scattered on the grass, some jutting out of or floating on the shallow lake created by the flood, along with roof panes and planks that had been torn off the house and barn. In the scars dug by the flooding in the gravel between the buildings water still ran, beneath small overhangs of soil that threatened to collapse. A red and yellow toy lay muddied and squished against the corner of the ramp to the silo tower. The air smelled of mud and smoke.

Along the path to the cabin the vegetation had been flayed, revealing soil or jagged bedrock where the earth had been washed out into the ditch on either side of the trail. In the fields that flanked the path, water was no longer frothing and churning, but stood still and dark like a new sea. The winter wheat had been bunched up into uneven, lopsided stacks, then flattened from every direction, or stood snapped with the head in the water. It looked like someone had gone over the stalks with a broad, dull scythe, harvested nothing, yet trampled everything. From where he stood he couldn't see a single square meter that wasn't broken or drowned. Even if the water drained from the fields, there would be no crop this spring. And who could say what the weather would be like the following winter, or when the next flood would come? Their project was over. When he realized that, his feet stopped by themselves on the disarrayed, overturned substrate, and he covered his mouth with his hand.

He feared that the cabin had collapsed either from the wind or runoff from the nearby hill, even if the cabin stood some distance away from its slope. As he passed the slight dip in the path where it started to curve up toward the cabin, the fog thinned sufficiently to see the red-painted structure. At least it was still there. He hurried the rest of the way, his breath catching in his throat.

The door was still in its frame, but hanging askew on the

upper hinges, with the bottom of the sun-bleached wood brown with mud. The deck was littered with grass, leaves, and branches from the hill. He kicked the worst of the debris away from the door and stepped over the rest. Inside the cabin's single room the water had smashed through the panorama window on its way back to the heather. Some of the glass remained on the floor by the gaping opening, the rest had scattered like a glittering stream on the mud outside. The walls were moist and spattered like the cliffs in a river gorge, and banks of dirt and vegetation had been deposited along them. In the northwest corner the rain had leaked in through the roof and streaked the wall with moisture. A small stream still trickled on the hardwood floor, filling the hearth with mud. The sofa lay outside the window, overturned and at an awkward angle, and the middle cushion sailed further afield. His small backpack and sleeping bag lay soaked in the east corner, just inside the broken glass. Of his treadmill, laptop, and mattress there were no signs; he assumed they were buried in the shallow flood lake somewhere. Only the kitchen had escaped substantial damage. The stove and the sink were still in place, but when he turned the faucet on it trembled and spat only brown water. The well must have been flooded too. He opened the powerless fridge. Inside the rubber-sealed darkness his phone and wallet lay dry and safe on the shelf where he had left them.

He took out the phone and was surprised to see that it still had service, although a barely detectable signal. At the edge of the drowned hearth he sent a short note to Michael, saying that he loved him and that he hoped everyone at home was all right after the hurricane. Then he deleted the email account, the phone's contact list, and reset the phone to factory settings. Finally, he dialed Kaye's number and texted a single word: "Yes."

36

FURTHER NORTH ALONG THE COAST SAT A POWER
plant, the spider in the center of a web of gently curving power
lines held aloft by a forest of steel pylons, every tenth tower
reinforced to prevent the ice in winter storms from pulling them
down. The plant was large enough to provide the region with
electricity, but not new enough for modern coal scrubbing methods, or important enough to have advanced security measures.
Instead, it seemed to have been partly left to anonymity and
civil obedience not to obstruct the giant and its humming supply
of power and normality. There had been plans to decommis-
sion the plant for years, but the public dislike of nuclear power
and the lack of properly developed alternatives, coupled with a
sharp increase in the price of power from abroad, no matter the
source, secured the single largest emitter of greenhouse gases
along that part of the coastline a continued existence.

Kaye had blueprints, door codes, key cards, showed him everything they needed to do, in the illumination from a single light
bulb in the basement of a house that was identical to all the
others in the streets and courts and crescents around it, all of
them empty and unused, owned by a financial institution that

was holding out for better times and higher prices that never seemed to happen.

He walked there with the hood of the sweater beneath his short wool coat up to shield him from the gaze of surveillance cameras on the train station, bus station, and the bus. The sky was white and heavy and the cold wind flurried with snow flakes, several months late for Christmas. The roads south were still closed, and air and rail travel there suspended, to the rage of the crowds of passengers now stuck on other parts of the continent. However, north of the hurricane's path of destruction, life continued more or less like before, with travel interrupted for only a few days after the disaster. He didn't expect to hear anything from Michael or Katsuhiro until phone and internet communication was restored.

The neighborhood in the northern city he traveled to had been developed, but not yet inhabited, so there was no bus nor tram line close to the address Kaye had texted him. He exited the bus at the nearest possible stop, crossed the road and an incomplete sports field with an expanse of newly planted, but already yellowed grass. Even here signs of recent bad weather were clearly visible: drains clogged with branches, fresh cracks and pot holes in the road, roof tiles and wayward planks on the pavement. The seating in the putative arena had only been partly completed, leaving broken scaffolding and plastic nets scattered about, torn loose by the elements. The evening wind rose and shrieked through the unfinished structure.

Past the sports field the residential streets were flanked by small gardens with gable-roofed, semi-detached houses in various stages of completion. The first properties were unfinished, lacking roofs or top floors, with pallets of shingles and paving still wrapped in plastic in the driveways. Further inside the neighborhood the houses had been roofed, painted a peachy yellow, and equipped with white Palladian windows in the fronts, showing off hardwood-floored halls and stairs inside. A few of the future homes even had brass chandeliers shining behind the windows and cone-shaped juniper bushes bounding their gardens, but no curtains, furniture, nor cars, so he assumed those buildings were marketing displays for selling. He wondered, if he continued in the same direction, whether the houses would become more and more inhabited, until rooms furnished with beds, closets, and chairs, tables set with meals, tubs filled with water, and hallways cluttered with shoes and clothes would appear, like landlocked ships abandoned by their owners. Or had he already reached the apex and the properties further in would only be less complete, with the roofs, walls, and floors vanishing in an inverted sequence from the structures he had already passed, until only concrete foundations and the burrows created by rock blasting to cradle them were all that was left of the houses? He had no desire to witness that and did not plan to walk further into the neighborhood than he had to, yet nevertheless experienced a small flash of regret knowing that he would never see what the houses farther inside looked like and that he might never return to find out.

Daylight lingered for much longer than in the depths of winter, but the milky sky remained opaque and dusk arrived as a jaundiced glow above the rooftops. This far into the residential area the streets were named and the houses numbered, enabling him to find the address he had memorized.

The house was identical to all the others: peach-colored, gabled roof, Palladian window, double garage. In the modestly sized garden, instant lawn had been laid out, some rolls only half way or still constricted by plastic string. A small pool yawned in concrete, holding no water, only sand, pieces of greasy plywood, and brown and yellow leaves. The house looked finished, but the one behind it had all its windows broken, dark shards gleaming in the patchy lawn. Past that structure torn tarpaulin was whipping in the wind, like prayer flags above a desolate mountain pass.

The white six-paneled, brass-handled front door was unlocked and led into a spacious hall lit only by the fading illumination from outside. The floor was tiled with textured, honey-colored ceramic rectangles and the walls painted a standard eggshell shade. The interior was new and unused, but dust had settled on every surface, like snow, and the stale, musty air signaled that the house had skipped past habitation on its way to dereliction. Every single house for at least a kilometer in all directions was as empty and abandoned as this. It was like being in a desert.

In the back of the hall a door-less opening and a short flight of stairs led down to the basement. Here, walls and floor-covering were in place, but had not been spackled or painted. Like the rest of the house the basement had already acquired the tang of decay. A single light bulb illuminated the subterranean space and he was not surprised to find Kaye, dressed in a thick down parka, waiting for him there.

Standing over Kaye's plans, which were laid out on a table improvised from a piece of drywall on two fuzzy sawhorses, they looked like new homeowners trying to agree on which task to tackle first. But their business was less constructive and required much more care.

"You're a bit late to join in the preparations," Kaye said, "but with your prior experience I'm certain you'll manage to keep up."

Kaye told him everything, and he confirmed that he had retained the information by reciting it from memory. During his brief narration of the story Kaye desired, the assistant professor nodded approvingly, as if he were listening to a graduate student verifying observations or recounting a long-established theorem, something that had already become reality.

He glanced at Kaye and although he imagined that his horror must be fully visible on his face, the assistant professor said nothing. Kaye only met his eyes calmly, as if he knew, as if any resentment was safe with him, inside their now mutual, monumental secret.

Finally, Kaye handed him a new mobile phone and told him not to use it, only to keep it on and charged, and remain ready for the call that would come "in a matter of days." Then the assistant professor lifted a dark leather bag onto the makeshift table and zipped it open. It had been years since he'd smelled the scent of oil and propellant which rose from the glistening, disassembled object inside, yet he recognized it instantly.

"This is yours," Kaye said. "We will most certainly need it, so take good care of it."

He stood numb, his thoughts a tangle, his worst fears having been confirmed all at once, and with it the vertiginous knowledge that the outcome he had tried so hard to avoid had finally caught up with him.

Kaye looked at him. "The others and I respect you immensely," the assistant professor said. "We asked you to join us because we trust you and want you here. We, I, want you with us." Kaye put his arm around him. "We're all together in this. All right?"

"Yes," he said, but could not meet Kaye's eyes.

37

HE CARRIED THE BAG FROM KAYE WITH HIM BACK
to the center of the unfamiliar northern city, the weight of its
contents as familiar as that of a lover sleeping on his arm. He
considered not opening the bag, not looking at the object inside,
not cleaning it, not testing it, since he didn't wish to use it. But
then he thought of how, if he refused to familiarize himself
with the gift, it might be him missing and the other person aiming true instead, and something in him was too proud to let that
happen because of something as stupid as misguided reluctance.

Back in the city center he withdrew money from a cash
machine, bought a case of self-heating field rations and packets
of liquid energy gel, hired a car with a hybrid engine under an
assumed name, and drove in the direction he had first arrived
in. He had spotted the place from the train and taken note of it,
knowing what Kaye wanted. After a brief search in the forest-
filled darkness he pulled into the parking lot and stopped the
car, checked that all the windows were up and the doors locked,
before he lowered the driver's seat as far as it would go and went
to sleep.

During the night, he woke several times, turning in the cold,
pulling the coat tighter around himself. The last time was at

dawn, when a gray mist rolled in between the trunks of the slim, ancient-looking firs that stood in front of the car. The fog pulled his gaze in, capturing his attention completely, and then it was like he could see the entire forest, row upon row of firs all the way back to the first tree. His pulse beat slowly in his ears, but behind it hummed a silence that engulfed him. He fell into a deep sleep and didn't wake till it was nearly midday.

Only a few other vehicles occupied the parking lot, a gravel-covered rectangle overlooking the narrow but fast-flowing river that wound through the valley. It was known as a great place for trout fishing, and he half expected to see fly fishers casting their lines on the banks, but there were none. He got out, locked the car, yawned and stretched, and walked to the edge of the gravel. The day was windless, but a fine rain hung like a curtain in the air. In the middle of the river was a small shrub-covered islet and a few boulders downstream. On both banks the remains of small birches and bird cherry trees leaned over the water, whose surface was smooth and glassy, even from where he stood. The vegetation on the bottom of the river looked like green hair that streamed and fluttered with the current. On the bank below the parking lot stood the red and yellow posters he had spotted from the train.

He took the bag carefully out of the trunk and crunched across the gravel to the steel-paneled building on the other side of the rural road. Inside the entrance a teen in thick coveralls and boots sat behind a fold-out plastic table with a red steel box and a school textbook open in front of him.

"Member or non-member?" the boy said.

"Non-member," he said.

"We're offering a discount on yearly memberships," the boy started, barely looking up from the book. "It gives better hourly rates..."

"That won't be necessary," he said. "I only need access for today."

The boy nodded. "Want to buy ammunition?"

"No, but I'd like to borrow ear protection and sandbags, if you have them."

"We have good muffs and bags," the boy said. "They're right inside."

"Thank you," he said.

The boy mentioned a small sum of money. He handed the boy a note, told him to keep the remainder, then strode past him and into the building.

A wooden deck shielded by a strip of moss-thatched roof looked out on a wide field of short grass and circular targets. He walked to the end of the gallery, past the few people who were already there, hunched down, and opened the bag. The smell of oil and metal rose from it and mixed with those of his surroundings: gunpowder, wood varnish, moist grass, and rain. He took out the cleaning kit and inspected its brushes, rod, screwdrivers, and cleaning solution for the first time.

Fortunately, whoever had made the purchase had wrapped and packed the gun properly. The weapon itself had been disassembled and was rolled up in a soft, dust-free cloth. The finely measured and manufactured parts glistened of oil, the barrel and chamber shiny and unused. He went through every item, cleaned and oiled them, then put them together into the whole they were meant to form, hesitating a little with the trigger mechanism for not having previous experience with the manufacturer. The scope and mount, however, was a brand he was familiar with, although the make was new to him, and they immediately clicked into place.

Beyond the shelter of the moss-covered roof, the rain fell unceasingly, creating a low hiss in the grass. He had no time to lose. The midday light was gray and even, but would soon give way to dusk. He put the ear protection muffs on, took out his phone, removed and folded his coat, and placed both next to the bag. Then he lay down prone with the rifle on the sand sock and aimed at the nearest target. There were no flags or markers up, but judging from the curtain of precipitation, the wind speed must be close to zero. He looked through the scope, its aiming reticle and dots black and clear, leaned into the stock, and relaxed. The focus and breathing technique he had been taught returned immediately. When he was comfortable he took the first shot.

A few more rounds told him that the parts were working well and made him familiar with the trigger pressure needed. He then shot to calibrate the optics at one hundred meter range, tapped the results into the phone between each shot to characterize the weapon, like a naturalist describing the individuals of a new species. After each shot he checked the lip of the barrel for the golden mark of copper traces, cleaned and oiled it, and set it to cool. When the sights were giving consistent results, he repeated the calibration and cleaning procedure at three hundred meters and then at a range of five hundred meters. The weapon and optics seemed stable and sufficient. The barrel coppered slightly, but not so much that he couldn't get rid of it with the equipment and cleaning solution that was in the bag. He shot five series of five more rounds, letting the weapon cool after each shot, cleaning the barrel and lubricating the bolt after each series. He wondered if the rain might cease or the wind pick up as evening approached, but the droplets remained a vertical drapery and the grass stood straight and unmoving as the afternoon progressed. He cleaned the rifle again, then shot five series of five rounds each, to see how the weapon behaved when it was warm. When those results became predictable and repeatable, he made a few final shots, cleaned and oiled the rifle one last time, before he rolled it into the cloth and returned it to the bag, together with the rest of the equipment. Night had fallen and the fluorescent lamps in the roof blinked on. When he passed the table in the entryway it was empty, and he hurried to leave before anyone else appeared.

At the car he put the bag in the trunk, vomited into the grass at the edge of the gravel and spat into the vegetation. Then he started the vehicle, drove it back to the rental agency in the center of the northern city, and fetched his backpack at the train station. From there the trip on the night train south to the mountains was long and silent, and ended with him walking back from the platform to the cabin in the faint beam from the headlamp, not feeling his legs nor hands nor feet, not even the weight of the bag held close to his body.

He put the backpack and the bag in the corner of the cabin that had the least amount of water on the floor, went back outside and walked to the grove of birches that separated Eloise and Mark's land from his. In the scattered light from the headlamp the trunks were speckled black on silver, the bark rough and grainy. The trees were slim and only a little taller than himself, kept low and humble by the altitude and wind, not like in the lowland where deciduous trees grew to three times that size. The birches even bent in the same direction as the most prevalent motion of air. The ground was covered by the leaf-fall from the birches, heart-shaped yellow, orange, and brown foliage that had survived the mild winter. He lay down, the beam from the lamp bobbing with his motions, and breathed in the fragrance of decomposition and soil, letting the earth's moisture seep into his clothes, while earthworms, beetles, and slugs crawled over his face and hands.

38

INCLUDING KAYE THEY WERE SIX, STANDING ON the beach inside the night. The early spring wind was sour and chilling, but had already lost its winter teeth. He regretted not having said goodbye to Michael properly after Christmas, one last moment of tenderness between them to pretend he wasn't the kind of person who would do what he was about to.

Kaye had texted him on the phone he'd given him in the basement of the empty house, telling him to take the train back to the city in the north where they had met, walk to a particular beach, and crush the phone on the way. It was just a few weeks since he met Kaye in the unfinished neighborhood, but it felt like years. During the time waiting in the cabin for the message he knew would come, and on the journey to that beach, he had been torn between what he thought was necessary and what he knew was right, the future and the past. As when he had first arrived at the cabin, he yearned to call Michael and flee back to the city.

He glanced at the others, thought he recognized Narayan and the blond woman from the second lecture, but wasn't certain. He took in what he could see of their faces, the eyes and forehead and hair, trying to imagine what they looked like beneath the thin fabric of their masks. In the low illumination he couldn't even see the shade of their eyes, whether they were light or dark, much less the color. If their features had been fully visible, he could have guessed what they looked like as children or would when they grew old, perhaps even when they were dead.

"It's time," Kaye said and waded into the inflatable vessel that was bobbing in the surf. The others followed. Despite the coveralls, masks, and gloves Kaye had given them, he felt naked, exposed. The engine roared to life, spewed exhaust fumes, jolted the small craft to motion. One of the four strangers startled visibly, the others remained calm and passive.

The craft kicked up sprays of seawater as it sped across the surface. The vessel had been following the beach for less than ten minutes and they were no farther than a kilometer from land, but the gleaming shore, with its weekend vacationers, surf and turf dinners, and off-season specials, seemed a million light years away.

Yet, even now the impulse to resist was strong, like pulling his hand away from a hot plate, or closing his eyes before a punch. Scenario after scenario that suggested a way, no matter how unrealistic or risky, out of the current situation, surged through his mind. The solutions offered were so tempting that his body swayed with the desired motion. For a while he defused the impulses before they could turn into action, but suddenly, he could no longer stop the urge that rose in his spine, could no longer stand the choking feeling in his throat, despite how things were and how he felt about them. In the past he had had similar doubts and not acted on them because the cost seemed too high, but now he no longer had a choice.

"I can't do this!" he shouted over the din of the engine and the noise of the wind. "I'm sorry."

The others turned toward him as if they were taking him in

from a far distance, but the vessel didn't slow down. He wasn't even certain they had heard him over the motor noise and the emptiness of the water. Quickly, he leaned over the rubber side of the craft, as he had been taught to in case of emergency evacuation, but never had to do before now, curled up into a ball to protect his head and chest, and launched himself into the roaring blackness.

He hit the water hard, bounced once along it like a skipping stone, and for a frightening moment he thought he would keep going, but then his motion slowed enough for the ocean's surface to soften and take him in.

He let himself sink into the dark, still curled up, struggling not to gasp from the cold water that rushed into his nose and ears and clothes. He wondered if the rubber vessel would turn to search for him, but he thought not. Their window of opportunity was limited, and he had shown himself a traitor before they had even started. Still curled up, he blinked against the cold water, tugged at his boots with slow, deliberate motions to make the oxygen he had last longer. He expected resistance, but the boots came off even though his fingers were growing stiff from the chill. The water must have softened the lining. The rifle was gone, it no longer hugged his body. He imagined it falling through the water, sailing back and forth like a black feather, before being swallowed up by the deep. He kicked to get to the surface while he pulled the top of the coveralls off.

He had just enough air to stop for a few seconds to listen for the sound of nearby engines before he broke the surface. There was none, only a low, distant hum that vanished quickly in the wind and the waves. He scanned the darkness for the telltale motion of the lightless vessel, but saw nothing. Staying low in the water, he discarded the coveralls, then began to swim toward land.

At first the water was warmer than he had mentally prepared for when he left the craft. He had expected muscle cramps from the chill, but that didn't happen. It was cold, but not as cold as it would have been that early in the spring a few years back. The wind had picked up and lashed the surface white, but it hadn't been blowing for long, so the waves were still manageable. The water was still cool enough to chill him and the piercing wind made his ears ache.

He hoped they assumed he had drowned, but he nevertheless glanced back several times. After about forty-five minutes of swimming at medium speed to pace himself, the cold began to bother him. It had been a long time since he had swam in the sea in early spring, and when he did he had worn a wetsuit. The salt burned his eyes, blurred his vision and forced itself into his nose and mouth. His right hand, whose bones still bore plates and screws after his visit to the abandoned asylum last spring, turned stiff and aching. The shore was still far away.

He used to think that when people drowned they behaved like sinking characters in films or on TV, splashing and yelling and waving their arms. But during his training he learned that people who were about to drown were quiet and exhibited little motion. He had assumed that was due to embarrassment and an erroneous belief that they would manage to get out of the trouble on their own, but according to the instructor, this was caused by the nature of drowning itself. Drowning victims were running out of air even if they managed to keep their mouth above the surface. In medical terms, drowning was slowly suffocating from lack of oxygen; it wasn't just getting water in the lungs.

Were the wind and the current taking him away from land? He gulped and snorted, trying to get rid of the water in his mouth and nose, but his breathing, which had started controlled and regular, had become more and more imbalanced. Every time he thought he was on the up stroke and had his chin above water, a wave arrived and splashed him in the face, forcing him to swallow mouthfuls of sickening seawater. He gagged and coughed and spat, but soon a coppery flavor told him his nose was bleeding from the salt and the force of the waves, while all the muscles in his body hurt from straining against the sea.

He started to wonder whether drowning was the end that had been chosen for him, that he would be devoured by the deep as easily as the rifle, by an element he had always felt comfortable, even intimate, with. But as he swallowed the last mouthful of seawater he thought he could take, completely out of breath, and knew he had reached the limit of his endurance, he saw that the lights on the beach were substantially closer. He continued to reach for them, with one more stroke, and another, and another. His hands and feet were stiff from cold, blood running down his face, while he was dog-paddling more than swimming. He put all his focus on keeping air in his lungs for buoyancy. Then the ocean roared and roiled and he felt it swell behind him, like the maw of a Kraken about to rise up from the deep. The motion surged his body forward, and there was no resisting or refusing being engulfed. Realizing his complete and utter helplessness, he gave in to the sea the same way he did with the inner brightness and let it carry him where it wanted to.

The long wave didn't crash or slam him back into the water, but crested gently without foam, then threw him up on land like a distasteful meal. It even pushed him a little into the cold sand, so that when the surf finally receded back into the ocean, he was left lying in a depression shaped like his own body, too exhausted to even cough.

39

THE OCEAN NIPPED AT HIS TOES AND SPLASHED his feet and ankles, each new wave renewing the intensity of his shivering. An icy wave rolled as far as his crotch, causing him to gasp and open his eyes. He pushed his hands and knees beneath him and stumbled up. The beach tilted back and forth and his ears were ringing with pain. His arms and legs were stiff and ached from freezing. He was so cold it felt like he'd never stop shaking.

The beach and the slope up to the road were still a wall of darkness ahead, but behind him the sky had started to pale. At the horizon the dawn had broken through the clouds and silhouetted them against the blue of the pre-dawn sky. The knowledge that he must not be seen took over and pushed him onward.

Above the beach the hill had been sectioned into small communal gardens, separated by low hedges of boxwood and spirea. Each garden held a modest building, sheds or greenhouses he thought at first, but as he drew closer they turned out to be small wooden cabins painted in warm primary colors. The walls of the miniscule structures were covered in trellises and vines of climbing plants. Most plots had rows of vegetable or flower beds, but he also spotted a faux marble fountain and a sleeping brass fawn. The patchwork of gardens was protected by a chain-link fence, but a shed leaned against it in the corner by the gate. He followed the fence to the shed, climbed the chain-link, and landed on the roof. From there he jumped into the damp grass.

He assumed the communal garden was used mainly in the summer, but some owners might have started working on their crops early, so he had to be quick. Further in among the hedges and less visible from the road, he tried the doors and windows of each cabin, shed, and greenhouse. But the cabin doors were locked and no window was ajar in the early spring weather; some of them were still shuttered. Most of the sheds and greenhouses were locked as well, some with recent padlocks and chains, and those that were open offered only tools, seeds, and fertilizer.

After having tried several doors and helping himself to some soft winter apples from a cardboard box in a greenhouse, he finally found an unlocked shed. The space inside was long and narrow, with shelves made from simple planks, stacked with old cans of nails, screws, paint, and wood varnish, as well as plastic containers with herbicides and rat poison. A broom, hoe, and rake leaned against the shelves. On the floor was a paint-spattered high-pressure water cleaner and a plastic bucket. Behind the door hung a blue janitor's coat, a pair of wide cotton shorts, and a sweatshirt full of white paint stains. Beneath them stood two orange plastic clogs and two navy rubber boots. He took all the clothes and the rubber boots outside with him and pulled them on with shivering hands. The clothes were too large to fit well, but not too wide to move in. The coat smelled of weed killer and sun lotion, a summer world a universe away.

In the town center the streets were empty and damp from rain. The store windows were so dark they seemed incapable of reflecting the morning light. Even the train station was unlit and closed. He squatted in a corner of the platform, trying to get away from the wind that was always high this close to the sea. On the other side of the rails aspen and rowan trees stood yellow, as if it were still autumn. He trembled with cold, and now that he was beginning to get his breath and thoughts back, he was both thirsty and hungry.

He worried that the first train would be a commuter train and that the station might get crowded, but when the train finally arrived the space was nearly empty. Only a few other people were waiting, hunched inside their clothes, looking more asleep than awake. He let them board first, they entered different cars, then he snuck in behind them. He went straight to the bathroom, closed the door quietly without turning the lock, and pulled the toilet lid down to sit on and keep his feet away from the floor. Despite a deep, pulsing thirst, he didn't dare turn the faucet on even after the train started moving, as he feared the pipes might rattle, signaling that the bathroom was in use. Neither did he dare crank up the tiny radiator beneath the window, in case it too would make noises as hot water flowed in.

Unhurried footfalls were approaching in the hallway outside and he held his breath, but the conductor didn't try the door, and he finally started to settle. After a while the warmth in the bathroom and the clacking of the wheels became so sleep-inducing that he had to get up and stand, away from the window. At every stop he heard steps outside and leaned against the door, but all of them passed by. After several hours, right before his station, he rushed up, ran the faucet without worrying about the sound of the water and the trembling of the pipes, and drank his fill of the metallic, lukewarm fluid.

The worn train platform on the moor was empty as usual. During the walk back to the cabin, he noticed that he had stopped shivering and that his hair was almost dry. He took out a wrinkly winter apple from the pocket of the old coat, rubbed it between his palms and bit into it. The flesh was dry and sweetly overripe, but it was the best meal he had had in a long time.

In the ruined cabin he stuffed the stolen clothes into a plastic bag, changed into the t-shirt, running pants, and boots left after the flood, and started walking toward the lake in the east.

The still surface mirrored the blue mountains and the wall of firs that skirted the water. The sky was overcast but luminous, as when the sun is about to break through the clouds on a bright summer morning. The song from blackbirds and robins echoed across the shore, and somewhere among the trees a woodpecker beat out its signal. In the lake a gray heron shrieked and lifted from the surface. The air smelled of leaves, pine, and grass. He waded into the lake, the water so still he could see through the surface and down to the bottom. He continued until the stony substrate vanished and the water turned dark. There he threw the plastic bag as far out into the lake as he could. The bulging object gave up some bubbles, tilted slightly, then sank. Rings spread slowly on the surface, intermingled and merged, before the water smoothed again, like a sleeping mind after a nightmare.

He turned and waded back to where the water met the grass. There he pulled off the t-shirt and stepped out of the boots and sweatpants. He knelt in the shallow, fresh water and rinsed his hair and skin. There were red bruises on his left side, probably from the rifle, and scratches on his calves and thighs, perhaps from the chain-link fence and hedges in the communal garden. When he cleaned the cuts they bled a little, but not much. He scrubbed his face and neck and arms, and cried until it felt like all the salt had left him. Then he rinsed his mouth with the warm fluid, which tasted of moss and marsh and mud, but was infinitely sweeter than the cold and bitter sea.

40

HE DIDN'T CALL THE POLICE, DIDN'T NOTIFY THE authorities, didn't let anyone know. By now the attack would be over, whether Kaye and the others had succeeded, or the police and special forces had killed them. He didn't even feel the need to seek out a TV screen or a newspaper to find out what had happened. He only desired to listen to the silence that now burned inside him.

He slept for twenty-four hours in the dried-up sleeping bag on the floor, undisturbed and unvisited in the gaping remains of the cabin.

The next afternoon he was woken by the sound of footsteps on the deck. He jolted into consciousness and sat up, prepared for uniforms and guns, shouts and threats. Instead there was just Eloise's voice asking if he was home.

He breathed to regain composure before he shuffled over to the askance barrier and opened it. Eloise looked rumpled and harried, and behind her in the cold mist a sport utility vehicle filled to the roof with bags and clothes and children and a small dog, was idling. He steeled himself for a look of pity or incomprehension for his ruined domicile and a surprised, "Are you still here?" but Eloise's eyes were moist and distant.

When he and Beanie were students at the university and shared a drafty apartment in the old part of the city, Beanie had come home early from her part-time job in a large record store. The manager had been apprehended for helping himself to the cash in the till and it had been going on for weeks before other employees had noticed and called the main office. Beanie didn't say anything, only sat down on the futon in the living room. Now Eloise had the same expression of shocked finality.

"How are you doing?" he said, not knowing what else to say.

"Good, good," Eloise muttered. "Mark and I just wanted to, wanted to say goodbye before we left."

He wasn't surprised, but it nevertheless made him sad. "Are you leaving?" he said.

Eloise nodded. "We have to. The farm has been in our family for generations, but we have no money to rebuild with. Everything we had went into the project. The bank is foreclosing." Eloise's voice was quiet and even.

"I'm terribly sorry," he said.

"So am I," Eloise said, gnawing on the nail of her ring finger.

"Where are you going?" he said.

"Family up north. The roads finally opened. We'll stay a while with them, just to regain our balance. Who knows where we'll go from there. And you, have you heard from your family after the hurricane?" She looked at him as if she was seeing him for the first time since he opened the door.

"I haven't gotten hold of them yet," he said.

"What will you do now?"

"I'll stay a while longer. Clean up a little. See if I can get in touch with my family."

"Good," Eloise said and reached out and rubbed his arm. Her eyes were red and swollen. "Thank you so much for being a part of our project. We had a meeting earlier this week, we wanted you to be there too, but you were away. We... we've closed it down and handed in our final report to the research institutions that funded us. The others are leaving too."

He hugged her and she cried a little into him, before she stood and wiped her face. "I'd better be going," she said. "Mark and the children are waiting."

"Good luck," he said. "Please send a card and let me know how you're doing."

"We will," Eloise said. "Oh that's right. I almost forgot." She rummaged in the pocket of her oilskin jacket. "The mailman stopped by to check who was still here. He asked if you had left, and since we weren't certain, he told us to give you this." The envelope Eloise held out to him displayed the logo of the space organization in bright, conspicuous color. "I hope you don't mind that we kept it for you."

"Of course not," he said. "Thank you so much."

"Well, goodbye then," Eloise said, shot him a pale smile, stuffed her hands into her pockets, and headed toward the waiting car. He remained on the deck until there was only the sound of the wind. The sky was gray and distant, as if it was about to snow, but the temperature was much too high for that.

He opened the envelope with trembling hands.

"Dear astronaut candidate," the letter began. "We deeply regret to inform you that the astronaut training program has been discontinued, without plans for restarting in the foreseeable future. Due to the recent catastrophic events along the coastline of our continent, the decision has been made at the ministerial level to refocus all our funding into research concerning the Earth and its climate and environment, leaving the exploration of the solar system the domain of robotic missions. Closing the manned space program saddens us all, but we hope it may be of consolation to know that you were close to being among our next class of astronauts. We encourage you to take a look at our vacant placements and current research opportunities and apply where appropriate. We thank you for participating in the testing and wish you the best of luck with all your future endeavors."

The letter ended with the signatures of the manager of the manned space exploration program and the head of the space organization itself.

He straightened and took in the muddy soil, the brown flood lake, and the broken stalks in the fields, the now abandoned farm across the plain, the smashed cabin, and finally, his own empty hands.

One can never truly possess anything, he thought, but even that notion seemed distant and inconsequential. The sensation of nothingness he had felt since the end of the previous summer was now stronger than ever. He was no longer in the picture, even if he could see his hands. No head, no body, no outside or inside — it was as if he had been replaced by the entire rest of the world. He had grown so used to the experience that he'd stopped thinking about it. Now he realized he would stay that way for the rest of his life.

He returned to the cabin, wrapped the sleeping bag around his body, and sat down by the hearth. The sand in the square pit was dark with moisture and most of the once bright and fine grains had been forced up and out onto the floor by the flood. Yet a small spring of water, barely lifting its head above the remaining sand, rose from the bottom of the pit. The fluid looked transparent, not like flood-water or sewage. As he watched, the source grew taller and broader until the water beneath it formed a small mirror where fire once had burned. It wouldn't afford him much warmth, but it would still his thirst, the first and foremost of all needs after air.

Dust and sand roiled like smoke in the breaths from the cracked door and the broken windows. Outside, the fields lay black and empty, with no one to till or sow them. The gray light of the day dimmed to a blue dusk and settled into distant, pale stars.

With thanks to François Bon, Jeremy P. Bushnell, Bill Campbell, Kevin Catalano, Patti Yumi Cottrell, D&C, Raechel Dumas and Jesse Bullington, Fábio Fernandes, Ignacio Gallup-Diaz, Kathy Fish, Jimin Han, Ian Sales, Paul Jessup, Jason Jordan, Kvalfangaren, Rochita Loenen-Ruiz, Michael Matheson, Mike Moore, my family, Eliza Wood-Obenauf and Eric Obenauf, Joseph M. Owens, Valerie Polichar, Edward J. Rathke, Sam Rasnake, Ethel Rohan, Donald van Deventer, and Ann and Jeff VanderMeer.

THE ONLY ONES A NOVEL BY CAROLA DIBBELL

"Breathtaking. It's that good, and that important, and that heartbreakingly beautiful." —NPR

"Fascinating... A heart-piercing tale of love, desire and acceptance." —*Washington Post*

HAINTS STAY A NOVEL BY COLIN WINNETTE

"In his astonishing portrait of American violence, Colin Winnette makes use of the Western genre to stunning effect." —*Los Angeles Times*

"A success." —*Washington Post*

SOME THINGS THAT MEANT THE WORLD TO ME
A NOVEL BY JOSHUA MOHR

* **One of the Best Books of 2009** —*Oprah Magazine*, The Nervous Breakdown

* *San Francisco Chronicle* **Bestseller**

"Mohr's prose roams with chimerical liquidity." —Boston's *Weekly Dig*

THE CORRESPONDENCE ARTIST
A NOVEL BY BARBARA BROWNING

* **Lambda Literary Award Winner**

"A deft look at modern life that's both witty and devastating." —*Nylon*

"*The Correspondence Artist* applies stylistic juxtapositions in welcome and unexpected ways." —*Vol. 1 Brooklyn*

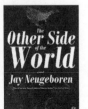

THE OTHER SIDE OF THE WORLD
A NOVEL BY JAY NEUGEBOREN

"Epic... *The Other Side of the World* can charm you with its grace, intelligence, and scope... [An] inventive novel." —*Washington Post*

"Presents a meditation on life, love, art, and family relationships that's reminiscent of the best of John Updike." —*Kirkus Reviews*, Starred